DO YOU HAVE A FAVORITE AUNT?

EDWARD DOESN'T.

"To be sure Aunts of all kinds are damned bad things."

—Oliver Goldsmith

"Many a man has dated his ruin from some murder or other that perhaps he thought little of at the time."

—Thomas de Quincey

A most unpleasant murder . . . but a very funny novel!

THE MURDER OF MY AUNT

Richard Hull

A CRIME CLASSIC

INTERNATIONAL POLYGONICS, LTD.
NEW YORK CITY

MURDER OF MY AUNT
Third printing November 1985
10 9 8 7 6 5 4 3

A NEW INTRODUCTION

Don't read this introduction.

Richard Hull's THE MURDER OF MY AUNT is a novel filled with surprises, and I really wouldn't want to spoil them for you.

Aha!, says you. Then why did you write an introduction?

Oho!, says I. It's what I get paid for. It keeps the landlord off me back, old dear.

Besides, now I've got your attention . . . but remember, you've been warned!

THE MURDER OF MY AUNT is a classic example of the "inverted" detective story. As its name implies, the inverted story—usually told from the point of view of the criminal—is not a whodunit but a will-they-catch-him.

Most historians of mystery fiction credit R. Austin Freeman with originating the form in a 1912 Dr. Thorndyke novel entitled THE SINGING BONES. The beginning of this novel, I am told, gives a detailed description of the crime while the balance shows Thorndyke's use of his famous scientific methods to bring the villain to justice. Maybe the historians are right. Maybe not, for although I have no idea if Dostoyevski ever read a detective story, I'm willing to bet that quite a few mystery novelists have read CRIME AND PUNISHMENT.

Unfortunately the term "inverted story" is used rather broadly and has encompassed everything from Freeman's stories to some of Grahame Greene's early "entertainments" and includes Dreiser's AN AMERICAN TRAGEDY. Furthermore, that most overworked mystery sub-genre, the caper novel, is an offshoot. The best recent examples of the inverted form were Levinson and Link's brilliant television series COLUMBO.

A more precise definition of the inverted detective story is impossible. Like pornography, you know it when you see it.

Two prime examples of the inverted story which are a far cry from Freeman's work are the major novels of Francis

Iles: MALICE AFORETHOUGHT (1931); and BEFORE THE FACT (1932) Frances Iles was one of the pen names of Anthony Berkeley Cox, who dropped his surname when he wrote THE POISONED CHOCOLATES CASE.

BEFORE THE FACT is better known, primarily because it was the basis for Alfred Hitchcock's film SUSPICION. Iles' title is taken quite literally: the novel is the story of a wife who suspects her husband is trying to kill her.

MALICE AFORETHOUGHT is much more interesting. A hen-pecked country doctor decides to do away with his wife. It is quite a good novel, marred only by a badly contrived ending for which the author has not laid the proper ground-work. If you decide to read it, skip the last page and a half.

Still the novel had many readers including a chartered accountant who had just failed in setting up his own practice. This fellow read MALICE AFORETHOUGHT and was so inspired by it that he decided to become a professional writer. The accountant's name was Richard Henry Sampson, but he used his mother's maiden name, which was Hull, as a *nom de plume*. THE MURDER OF MY AUNT by Richard Hull was published in 1934 in England and a year later in the States.

Hull told of this experience in the third person in a letter to the eminent mystery critic-historian Howard Haycraft:

It can't be said that he was ever a very successful accountant, and in 1935 he began to think that he would be more interested in writing. The decision to do so and to concentrate mainly on a particular type of detective fiction was made after reading Francis Iles' MALICE AFORETHOUGHT.

Hull's memory for dates is imprecise. In 1935 he had already had his second novel published. Perhaps his recollection of his influences isn't any better. You see THE MURDER OF MY AUNT has almost nothing in common with MALICE AFORETHOUGHT save that they are both first-class inverted detective stories.

Both men wrote with humor, but Iles tends to be condescending toward his characters while Hull is flat out funny, a true comic novelist. Iles' novel is told in the third person— from the point of view of the murderous doctor; Hull's book —as the title indicates—is told in the first person by nephew Edward, a rather bizarre and definitely not impartial narrator. However, Hull's approach is an advancement of a technique used by Wilkie Collins in THE MOONSTONE and has nothing to do with Iles.

In fact the only real point of similarity in the two novels is that both have protagonists who view murder as an art form as did Thomas de Quincey, who in 1827 wrote "Murder as One of the Fine Arts", an essay which earned him a reputation among his contemporaries as a humorist. Here is de Quincey's advice to a servant in an 1839 addendum to his famous essay:

> If once a man indulges himself in murder, very soon he comes to think little of robbing; and from robbing he comes next to drinking and Sabbath-breaking, and from that to incivility and procrastination. Once begun upon this downward path, you never know where to stop. Many a man has dated his ruin from some murder or other that perhaps he thought little of at the time.

Iles' physician is depicted reading this essay before committing his crime. Nephew Edward has this to say of murder: "It will be a distasteful business, but in the cause of art, one must be prepared to make sacrifices. And I intend that my conduct, till this matter is over, shall be thoroughly artistic."

Then why does Hull credit MALICE AFORETHOUGHT with his decision to become a writer? Perhaps he was thinking of some rather light-hearted mysteries Iles had written under his real name A. B. Cox, but I suspect that he didn't like the ending of MALICE AFORETHOUGHT either.

The truth is that Hull is pretty much of an original. Innovators in most fields tend to be controversial, and the mystery novel has had its share of icon-breakers. Agatha Christie aroused the wrath of readers when they discovered the murderer of Roger Ackroyd. E. C. Bentley created a fallible detective in TRENT'S LAST CASE which would have been more controversial if most readers had not been lulled to sleep by one of the longest denouements in detective fiction.

THE MURDER OF MY AUNT drew fire on two counts. I won't discuss the first; you'll know it when you get to it. Hull's second effrontery was that he had written a novel with a repulsive narrator. That the narrator was literally grossly funny didn't help a bit. Such criticism is unfortunate for nephew Edward is a superb comic creation who is totally believable in the context of the novel.

The depiction of Edward also illustrates two unique qualities of the inverted tale.

First, the author of the inverted story has no need to keep the identity of the criminal a secret from the reader as does the writer of the traditional whodunit. Raymond Chandler once pointed out that the revelation of the murderer in any of the Christie novels with "big" endings always involved someone acting totally out of character. Conversely, the whodunit writer cannot afford to make his characters too realistic for fear of losing an element of surprise in having too obvious a villain. The writer of the inverted story has no such prohibitions and may write as realistically as possible. Well, maybe not too realistically as the second characteristic shows.

As I have mentioned before, most inverted stories are written from the point of view of the criminal. It comes as no surprise then that the reader may wind up empathizing with a distasteful character, an experience which can easily be rather distressing. A skilled writer knows this and tries to mute the experience. In MALICE AFORETHOUGHT Iles, by writing condescendingly of his characters, keeps them at arm's length. If Hull had not made Edward into such a buffoon, he would be unbearable.

But since when are the Great Detectives so lovable? Hercule Poirot may have been a bachelor by choice—but whose choice was it? And would you really want to play skittles with Nero Wolfe if he wandered into your local pub?

In any event, Edward delighted some readers and offended others which is why THE MURDER OF MY AUNT has its fans and its foes. Among the former is Howard Haycraft who included the novel in his "Definitive Library of Detective-Crime-Mystery Fiction" and who called it "a classic of its kind, an intellectual shocker par excellence."

Among the less enthusiastic is the respected novelist-critic Julian Symons who finds the book "labored." In his otherwise excellent history of the detective story, MURDER, BLOODY MURDER (U.S. title: MORTAL CONSEQUENCES), Symons goes so far as to reveal the ending of THE MURDER OF MY AUNT.

Boooooo! Hissssss!

Your editor is tempted to avenge Hull by herein disclosing the endings of three Julian Symons novels.

Don't worry: I won't. You see, I happen to like and respect the novels of Julian Symons. I also like and respect the novels of Richard Hull. Assuming my taste is consistent, Mr. Symons may have cause for concern.

Who was Richard Hull?

I don't know much about him, but he certainly was different.

Case in point: Richard Henry Sampson wrote mystery fiction using the pen name Richard Hull. In 1940 Richard Hull wrote a novel, MY OWN MURDERER, whose narrator is an extremely nasty piece of work named Richard Henry Sampson.

Sampson was born in London in 1896. He prepped at Rugby, and by the time he was eighteen, he had qualified for Trinity College, Cambridge. But the year was 1914, and instead of a scholarship, Sampson accepted an Army commission and served in France for the remainder of the Great War.

Demobbed, Sampson apprenticed himself to a firm of chartered accounts where he remained until he tried to set up his own practice. As you know, he met with success as a writer, producing fifteen novels in all, the last of which was published in 1950. Sampson died in 1973.

Sampson sent this description of himself to Howard Hay-craft:

> In fiction, he specialized in unpleasant characters be-cause he says there is more to say about them and that he finds them more amusing. In life, he pleads a kind heart as a set-off to an occasional flash of temper and an endless flow of conversation. For many years he has lived almost entirely in a London club [he never mar-ried], qualifying, as he says, as the club bore. He is con-vinced that his photograph would be detrimental to his sales.

An interesting footnote: the Hull novels are renowned for their first person narratives yet when Sampson wrote about himself he wrote in the third person.

All the Hull novels I have read have at least one thing in common: an author who took an obvious delight in surpris-ing his readers. The surprise may be as simple as the guide to Welsh pronunciation which opens THE MURDER OF MY AUNT. It may be as complex as the entire novel MURDER ISN'T EASY (1936). (I defy anyone who has only read the first half of this novel to predict what the second half will even be about.) By the way, the setting of MURDER ISN'T EASY, a small advertising agency, has such a high degree of verisimilitude that one would never suspect that it was written by a chartered accountant rather than a copywriter like the principal narrator.

In THE GHOST IT WAS (also 1936) Hull experimented with the whodunit, not altogether successfully. However, this uncharacteristic (for Hull) third person narrative does contain one of the very few butlers in detective fiction who is a legiti-mate suspect, and the only detective in perhaps all the litera-ture who enters the case solely to clear a ghost of a charge of murder.

THE MURDER OF MY AUNT is usually considered to be Hull's masterpiece and rightly so. Not only is it a straightfor-ward comic novel, but it is practically a primer on how to write an inverted detective story. To be sure the book is over forty-five years old, but it doesn't show its age. Oh, maybe a little of its humor now appears somewhat heavy-handed, and its denouement *does* go on just a bit, but otherwise it's almost perfect.

So what are you waiting for? Read the book!

And enjoy it.

Burke N. Hare
Editor

London
July 1979

The Murder of My Aunt

By RICHARD HULL

"To be sure Aunts of all kinds are damned bad things."
                                    —*She Stoops to Conquer*

1: *One Hot Afternoon*

MY AUNT lives just outside the small (and entirely fright-ful) town of Llwll. That is exactly the trouble. Both ways.

How can any reasonably minded person live in a place whose name no Christian person can pronounce? And I do maintain that "Llwll" is impossible. One would like to begin at the beginning, but with Llwll you don't. You have to begin just before the beginning, which is ridiculous. One writer tells me that "ll" at the beginning of a word is pronounced like "thl" with the "t" partially left out—a guide which is quite useless and impracticable. Another one recommends a slight click made at the back of the throat as if you were going to say "cl" but were prevented apparently by someone seizing you by the throat. All I can say is that if, whenever you are asked where you live, you seize yourself by the throat and start choking, it is apt to cause comment.

But even if you do start to say the word, you still have difficulty in going on. It is of course not a "w," it is more like a double "o," but with a slight trace of a "u"! The ex-clamation mark is mine, the author apparently thinking his sentence in need of no such qualification. However, having clutched your throat and spluttered slightly, you may then tackle the final "ll," and here at any rate is certainty. It is pronounced "lth." What a business for a word of five letters!

For myself, I usually pronounce it Filth. It describes the place.

Llwlll—no, on a recount Llwll—I need hardly say, is in Wales. Quite a lot of people guess that straight off. And a

3

more horrible place I have never seen. It is amazing to me
how many people admire the Welsh scenery, indeed, I am
always being told how lucky I am to live in such a beautiful
country-side. I cannot imagine what they see in it. Nothing
but silly little hills, very fatiguing to walk up and instantly
going down again, sodden damp woods, out of which, if I
do try to exercise my dog in them, I am instantly chased by
some keeper who says I am doing harm to his beastly
pheasants and stupid little grass meadows. Ugh! how it bores
me. Give me Surrey every time.

And the roads. Horrible, twisting little lanes, mostly covered with loose jagged flints, and often with steep banks so
that one can see nothing but the hedgerows of brambles and
wild roses and other such things, all with sharp thorns, as
you find if you try to break through the fence, and I might
add that if I do manage to make a gap, some officious person
always fills it up with barbed wire. But if by any chance
one is spared this prison-like bank and fence, what does one
see? Why, the same thing every time. Miles and miles of hills
and woods, all looking exactly the same. No man has ever
taken this meaningless jumble created by nature and made
anything of it. It wants forming.

But to go back to the roads. There isn't a stretch anywhere
in the whole country-side where I can drive my car at a
decent pace. Think of it! I don't suppose that any car has
ever been over thirty-five in the whole country. What a
feeling of relief it gives me when I can leave it all behind and
get onto Watling Street and can really let myself go with
the straight road stretching away to the horizon, none of
these wretched hills, and a good surface beneath me instead
of these awful Llwll roads, repaired by putting down a very
little tar and a very large number of sharp stones about the
size of a hen's egg, and leaving such traffic as there is to roll
them in, a process which takes several years.

As I look back at what I have written in order to relieve
my mind of what I feel of this awful place, I see I spoke of
"sodden woods." That was the right adjective. Never, never

does it stop raining here, except in the winter when it snows. They say that is why we grow such wonderful trees here which provided the oaks from which Rodney's and Nelson's fleet were built. Well, no one makes ships out of wood nowadays, so that that is no longer useful, and it seems to me that one tree is much like another. I'd rather see less rain, less trees and more men and women. "Oh, Solitude, where are thy charms?" Exactly so. I had much rather be rocked with alarms than dwell in *this* desolate place.

Trees and rivers; rivers and trees. There must be thousands of trees to every human being round here, and I should think that in a twenty-mile radius from here there must be more trout than men. And of all the tedious people, commend me to those who like trout—to catch, I mean, not to eat. *Truite meunière* is excellent—they do it best at Ciro's to my mind—but *truite meunerie*, or the miller's mode of beating the water with a flail for trout, is tiresome beyond words. The pun is apposite if a little far-fetched.

But though there seem to be some people, curious people to my way of thinking, or perhaps merely ignorant people who do not know the district, who seem to like the country-side, there surely can be no one who likes Llwll. There isn't anything really to be said for it. There really is very little to be said about it. It is just a collection of ugly red-brick houses, all very like each other and mostly in none too good a state of repair, with the inevitable river running down the middle of it, lying in a hole amongst the hills, all of which are exactly like each other, with a stone church on a mound on one side and several nonconformist chapels dotted about it. I have never discovered quite how many of these chapels there are. Indeed, I am always finding a fresh one, belonging apparently to a different sect, or should one say, a different religion? I don't know.

There is a high street. It has a post office, from which the letters are occasionally delivered and occasionally not—some grocers, dealing almost entirely in tinned food of the most elementary and obvious kind at fifty per cent more than the proper price; and some butchers, selling mainly New Zealand lamb, Danish bacon and Argentine beef, which is ridiculous in a country-side which, whatever its defects, is full of sheep —peculiarly stupid sheep—and very inquisitive pigs. However, what are you to expect with a government such as we have at present, though really I take so little interest in these things that I am not quite sure what kind of a government we have just now. However, the inhabitants of Llwll continue to buy tinned salmon and tinned apricots for a treat, and economize in order to do so by eating frozen meat and margarine while the neighboring farmer—but let us not talk of farmers.

There is a cinema. Not that I ever wish to go to a moving-picture entertainment; vulgar, common, unrefined things with slapdash business and horseplay taking the place of refined wit, with sticky slabs of sentiment made to do duty as a plot, with no artistic composition in their technique, no facing up to the problems of life, no new, no original thought or conception in them. Who ever heard of a film play by Wilde, or Pirandello, or Tchekhov? The idea is ridiculous.

But even if I did want to go to such an entertainment, I could not consent to be seen in the Wynne Picture House, so called after the family name of Lord Pentre, the principal landowner of the district. The seats are all so cheap that one may find oneself sitting next to almost anyone, and, apart from the fact that there are class distinctions, some of the agricultural workers do smell so.

But to return to Llwll. Except by car it is very difficult to return to Llwll, and still more so to my aunt's house. The branch line winds its way on from England into this barbarous country very slowly. I always imagine to myself—a pretty fantasy—that the engine is loath to go to anywhere so preposterous as Abercwm, the market town about nine miles from Llwll. At Abercwm it is necessary to get onto a light railway, and a more boring snail's progress than the hour taken to go those nine miles I do not know. I prefer to draw a veil over that journey.

2

I think I have said enough to convince any reader, if there ever is a reader of these notes, the reason for whose existence I will explain later on, that to live near Llwll is appalling. To live in my aunt's house is even worse.

It is a good two miles from the end of the ridiculous Llwll light railway to Brynmawr, and my aunt is the sort of person who, if possible, arranges things so that you have to walk those two miles. She particularly likes to manage things so that I have to walk them, simply because she knows quite well that I dislike walking at all times, and have an absolute hatred of the road to Brynmawr. Brynmawr, I understand, means "The Big Hill," silly name for a house but one that is well justified. After you leave Llwll, you go steadily uphill for a mile and a quarter, and what a hill! My aunt, after studying the ordnance map with great care, tells me that you have to go up just on six hundred feet, and apparently it is a good deal. I can well believe her, but these figures mean little to me. It is, however, typical of my aunt that she not only possesses many maps showing this revolting country-side in the greatest detail for miles round, but that she can apparently find some pleasure in staring at them for hours on end, "reading" them as she is pleased to say, and produc-ing from memory figures as to the height of every hillock near by. On the other hand, there are no road maps in the house of any use to you for motoring.

However, having ascended the six hundred feet or yards, or whatever it is, you find yourself, in the irritating manner of this country-side, instantly obliged to go down again in order that you may immediately go up once more. That last three-quarters of a mile is a brute; my aunt says it is beauti-ful; for myself, I only find it interesting as a test of my car, for although the gradients are, I believe, nothing very startling, the abrupt bends, particularly by the bridge over the brook at the bottom of the dingle, to use the local term,

add to the difficulty by causing one to start at almost dead
slow. But as to walking up it—

My blood boils when I think of the trick by which my
aunt forced me this afternoon to walk down to Llwll *and back
again*, quite unnecessarily.

It all started at lunch. I had finished reading *La Grotte
du Sphinx* in the morning, and was wondering what on earth
to read in the afternoon. Of course my aunt has nothing in
the house fit to read. It's full of Surtees and Dickens and
Thackeray and Kipling, and dreadful hearty people like that
whom no one reads now, while my aunt's taste in modern
novels runs to *The Good Companions, If Winter Comes,* or
that interminable man, Hugh Walpole. Of course I have
made my own arrangements—partly with the Next Century
Book Club and partly with an admirable little French Library
I found behind the British Museum. Some very amusing stuff
they send me at times.

Normally I take care never to be left to the resources of
my aunt's works of fiction, but somehow or other the expected
parcel had failed to arrive by the morning's post, owing, I
expected, to the incompetence of the local post office. It is
not a pleasant prospect to be book-less, and it was in no
cheerful frame of mind that I watched my aunt's small,
determined figure tramping up the hill from the bridge.
Really, I reflected, Aunt Mildred was a dreadful sight in her
country clothes. However, a few moments in the garden
would be pleasant, and I stepped out to meet her.

From half-way across the lawn she waved to me and
started yelling at me from twenty yards away—a disgusting
trick.

"You haven't been stewing in the house all morning on a
lovely day like this, have you?" she said, pushing back a too
youthful béret of a rather ugly shade of blue across her
graying hair. "It's perfectly gorgeous out. Do your pasty face
a lot of good if you got out a bit more."

I do hate my aunt's personal remarks. I could have made
a very obvious retort. It had not improved *her* complexion.

As it was, I contented myself with a glance at her florid, bourgeois apple cheeks, the red patches made worse by the unconcealed drops of perspiration on her forehead. I don't believe my aunt knows what powder is.

"It *is* very hot," was my mild answer. "Much too hot to enjoy walking, I should have thought, even for those who like spending their time that way."

My meaning was not lost on my aunt. To do her justice, it never is. She can be relied on to realize what lies behind one's words quite well, sometimes too well.

"Well, I may be sweating—" ("Really, Aunt Mildred," I interjected) "but it's less of a waste of time than reading some smutty French novel."

"My dear Aunt Mildred, *La Grotte du Sphinx* is not in the least as you put it" (I raised my eyebrows) " 'smutty.' "

"Well, I expect my nose is," was my aunt's irrelevant rejoinder. "You'll be late for lunch if you don't go and wash your hands now."

My aunt removed a burr from her shabby, nondescript blue-green tweed skirt, and started to march into the house.

"I don't suppose I shall take as long as you, dear," I murmured. I hate being treated like a child, and I think it annoys my aunt to be called "dear." My aunt, for all her lack of inches and her old clothes, swept regally into the house.

"By the way," said my aunt, after lunch had partly passed away in rather stony silence, "I met Owen Davies down by the Fron Wood this morning."

I detached a momentary interest from my gooseberry tart. Owen Davies is the local postman, but as to where the Fron Wood is, I have no idea. All these woods seem much alike to me.

"He told me," continued my aunt, taking an inordinate amount of brown sugar, "that there was a parcel of books in the post office from somewhere French, but that the label had partly come off. He thought that they might be for you, knowing, as he said, 'that Master Edward is the only person near here who does read such things.' " (My aunt saw fit to break into that hideous Welsh sing-song. I managed not to wince at the "Master Edward.") "Of course they *are* for you, but you'll have to go down to Llwll to get them. Now there," added my aunt triumphantly "is an excellent object for a walk for you."

"I have no intention of walking, thank you, Aunt Mildred. I expect they're heavy. In fact, probably your protégé Davies found them too heavy and was too lazy to carry them up. I should think that was extremely likely," I went on, warming to my subject. "Who ever heard of a gummed label coming off in the post? My friends, La Bibliothèque Moderne, are extremely careful."

"No doubt." My aunt laughed unpleasantly. "They don't want them back through the post in case, in making inquiries, the police read them, but you forget the Llwll light railway. You know all the roofs of its carriages leak, and probably the label got half washed away by yesterday's rain, and then torn."

"Much more likely that Davies deliberately tore it. He hates carrying parcels up here."

"Well, so would you. In fact, you dislike the very suggestion that you should walk down and do once what you make him do once a week."

"It's his duty. It isn't mine," I replied with dignity, passing my aunt the cheese.

"And does that make it more pleasant? I know, if I were he, I should hate carrying that sort of book about."

"He's paid for it, isn't he?"

Somehow this mere statement of fact seemed to annoy my aunt. She rose from the table at once.

"Of course it's nonsense pretending that Owen Davies tore the label, but anyhow I shall see that you do not get that parcel unless you walk down to Llwll."

"That I shall not do," I said. Apparently my aunt was forgetting my car. I retired to my own little room, which my aunt maliciously calls my boudoir, for a few minutes' sleep after lunch—a healthy habit, I find. I was glad to be able to leave my aunt in her present mood.

Sleep, however, I found would not come to me so readily as usual. One needs an absolutely untroubled mind to fall off easily, and my mind was not untroubled. It would be unlike my aunt to forget my car, although I had carefully refrained from mentioning it, and she had sounded very positive in her statement that she would see that I did not get my books without walking. A sudden horrible idea came into my mind. Was my aunt capable of sabotaging my car, my precious car? The very idea banished all thought of sleep. I went straight round to the garage. As I passed through the hall I heard my aunt telephoning. She was actually telling the postmaster at Llwll that I was anxious about the books, and would he please see that they were delivered to no one but me in person at Llwll. The postmaster, I gathered, promised that they should not leave Llwll except in my company. Now, I wonder if I can get that fellow into trouble for delivering an unaddressed parcel. I have always disliked him.

My aunt, though, was evidently taking trouble in the matter. I heard her start another call as I went, and, to my horror, I recognized the number of the local garage, a very indifferent and badly run business, but the only one in Llwll. I hurried out to La Joyeuse, my car. Fortunately my aunt's knowledge of car engines is small. She would be unlikely to break La Joyeuse up with a hammer or any crude means of that sort, and as for more delicate work, well, she simply wasn't capable. It was, however, with considerable relief that I saw it there, and apparently intact. I would go straight down to Llwll in it before whatever scheme my aunt had in mind had been matured. It was just about then that I remembered that I had been anxious to make some minor adjustments to the engine, and with that end in view, for safety's sake, I had let the petrol tank get practically empty, and had even gone to the trouble of siphoning out the little that remained. My aunt must have known this and have decided

in her innocence that this simple fact would prevent me from
using La Joyeuse.

Simple, yes. But how simple to defeat. First I tried the
doors of my aunt's car. I was not surprised to find them
locked. However, my aunt, I knew, kept some reserve cans
of petrol for emergencies, on which I had been relying for
refilling my tank. I could use them. I went to where they
were kept, but, to my surprise, the shed was empty. My aunt
must have hidden them. This was infuriating, but if my aunt
thought I was defeated so easily as that, she would soon
find she was mistaken. It was a pity I had wasted time after
lunch and so given her the necessary minutes to act. I saw
now I should have gone at once. However, I, too, could
telephone to the Wynneland Garage.

I reached the telephone just as my aunt was leaving it.
There was an unpleasant glitter in her eye, but I was glad to
see that there was also a certain amount of alarm on her
face. As far as I could see, she was pleased with her strata-
gem, but her manner seemed to imply that she had overlooked some detail which was giving her cause for alarm.
I should make it my business to see that the alarm mate-
rialized, so to speak.

I am no great friend of Herbertson, the proprietor of the
Wynneland Garage. He does not really know his job, and
unfortunately when it has come to repairing my car, I have
been compelled to show him up and take my custom elsewhere. However, for simple matters one had to deal with
him, and one such thing was petrol. I would not of course
give my aunt away to a tradesman, so I merely said that my
aunt and I had both unfortunately run out of petrol at the
same time. Would he send a man up with some?

To my surprise, he said he was sorry it couldn't be done.
Here was an unexpected difficulty, the genuineness of which
I found hard to believe. With an effort I swallowed my
pride and represented to him how helpless both my aunt and
I were in the circumstances. I even went so far as to ask
his assistance as a favor for both of us. On the whole I

thought it best to include my aunt, for whom Herbertson has a great respect, while he does not entirely appreciate me, of which on the whole I am glad.

"Sorry, Mr. Edward," came Herbertson's unpleasant voice —I wish everyone round here would not use my Christian name—"I haven't got anyone I can possibly spare. I would always do everything I could to help Miss Powell, but she was explaining the situation to me just now, and I gathered from her it wasn't urgent—and anyhow I'm very sorry, but I'm afraid it's impossible"—and with that he had the impertinence to ring off!

"I'll never spend a penny at his beastly place again, if I can help it," I thought, though for that matter that has been my attitude for a long time, and occasionally it is necessary to make use of his garage.

I sat for a moment in thought. Of course it was overwhelmingly clear that he was lying at my aunt's instructions. Very well then. My aunt had thought of my using that method to extricate myself and had defeated it. It was up to me to find another, for by now it had become a matter of pride that I should have those books and should not walk.

I could not then get petrol from the Wynneland Garage. Very well, I would get petrol from one of the garages in Abercwm! It would be expensive, but, to defeat my aunt, although I have not a great income, I was quite prepared to spend any amount. My aunt, too, would have the pleasure of paying for the telephone call to Abercwm!

But here a most unexpected hitch occurred. The line to Abercwm was out of order, and the operator had no idea when it would be right. Still, however, I refused to admit defeat. I would go on ringing up garages as far away as Shrewsbury, if necessary, but get petrol I would. I put out my hand for the telephone directory. It was not there. My aunt had hidden that too.

It seemed to me that my aunt had been pretty thorough. By now I expected that she had even got at the telephone operator. She has many local activities in Llwll, and knows everyone there, high and low, and probably is well aware who the girl is. For the moment I seemed to be defeated, but then I remembered the look on my aunt's face. There was something she had forgotten. For several minutes I sat and thought before at last it occurred to me. The doors of her car might be locked, but glass can be broken. There was petrol in her old Morris. The tank had been filled that morning. She must have been hurrying to take her car away as she should have done at first. I positively ran—and I never run if I can help it—to the garage. I might yet be just in time. Apparently I was; my aunt's car was still there.

But suddenly I became aware of a terrible strong smell of petrol. Now, my aunt's car, as I have mentioned, is an old Morris of positively prehistoric design. It is typical of my aunt that she scorns all modern inventions and continues to use this dilapidated old bus. I must admit that it still goes, and goes quite efficiently, but how she can bear to be so out of date, I cannot understand. Amongst the obsolete survivals of this car is its petrol supply. To empty the tank of my Wolsey Hornet completely, you have to siphon it out: to empty my aunt's, all you have to do is to remove the top of the float chamber. The result is that the petrol is not stopped in its flow and so just pours itself on the ground. And this is what my aunt had done, with the result that the last drain was rapidly trickling out. It was surprising that my aunt had known so much about her old Morris; she must have found it out accidentally some time last winter when she had had her float chamber cleaned after getting some water in.

But I had no time for speculation then. It was time to act. Grabbing the dog's drinking bowl and throwing away the water in it, I managed to save a little, a very little, of the temporarily precious fluid. It would, I hoped, be enough.

It was, however, very little. It certainly would not get me to Llwll and back, but I could buy some in Llwll—damn Herbertson—and that would be enough to give me victory. I looked at the drop of petrol again. It was doubtful if it would take me even to Llwll, but if it once got me over the dingle, I could run down the hill with the engine off.

It was indeed La Joyeuse in which I started. I was glad now I had not broken the windows of my aunt's car when I found it locked. I might have cut myself.

3

But it was not La Joyeuse in which I finished.

I got down to the bottom of the dingle, of course, and I nearly, oh! how nearly, got up the other side, but alas! I did not get to the top. The drop of petrol ran out some fifty yards too soon.

Now here really was a predicament. Obviously I could not leave La Joyeuse where it was. Equally obviously, I could not push her up the hill in front of me. It might have been possible to have pushed her back to Brynmawr, but it would have been extremely fatiguing, and besides, when I had done it, I was no farther on. For several minutes I stood looking at the car helplessly while an irritating bird made an idiotic noise in a bush near by and a stupid rabbit ambled across the grass at the bottom of the dingle. I stooped down and picked up a stone. It wasn't a bad shot and may well have hit the bird. Anyhow, it stopped its row, and the rabbit disappeared. I lit a cigarette to help my thoughts, and took a vow that my aunt should not have the pleasure of saying that she had forced me to walk into Llwll.

The form of the words gave me an idea. Somehow or other I had got to get out of the mess I was in. I could not let matters slide, for if my aunt found La Joyeuse where it was, her mirth would be intolerable. But if I walked the rest of the way to Llwll, bought some petrol, and came back to where I was, I could truthfully say that I had started in my car and returned in my car, and my aunt would never know she had succeeded in her spiteful object. I should of course have to walk most of the way there and back, but I should avoid the worst part of it all, namely, walking there *because my aunt told me to.*

The first thing was to hide La Joyeuse lest my aunt should come that way. I put her behind the nearest bush, an idea put into my head by the singing of that blackbird, which only goes to show that there is some use even in blackbirds. It was rather an energetic performance, and I was unpleasantly warm by the time I reached the crest. However, I loitered slowly down the road. It would never do to be seen hot and draggled in Llwll! As I went I thought out the way I could put it to Herbertson. In no circumstances would I let him know exactly what had happened. He would be certain to pass it on to that inveterate gossip, my aunt, a lady I might say who I have found from past experience is quite incapable of minding her own business or respecting anyone's privacy.

"Good afternoon, Herbertson." I assumed a pleasant air. If I had shown my feelings, he would have thought that his unobliging performance had put me out, and that would have pleased him as well as started a train of thought in his mind that I did not want. I wanted him to believe that it was all quite easy. "Glad you're so busy these days." Just to show how little deceived I was, I glanced round at his lounging assistants—"I found I had just a few drops of petrol after all. Just enough to get me within easy walking distance of you, so if you'll let me have a can of Shell I'll take it to the car and then I can go back easily."

"Within easy walking distance, Mr. Edward? I'll send a man to fill it up for you." His manner appeared more jovial than usual, but there seemed a curious twinkle in his eye.

"Oh, don't worry," I said. "I know you're too busy to spare a man, and it's no distance. I'll take it along myself. You need not worry about the can, I'll bring it back."

"That's all right, Mr. Edward. I know I could always charge you up for it if you didn't" (the commercial side of the man!), "but if it's no distance, I'll come along myself. I can spare a few minutes for an old customer," and with that the fat, red-faced fellow actually started to go on to the road as if he would walk with me to La Joyeuse! Not even in Llwll can I be seen walking along the road with a man in blue overalls. One has one's limits. Besides, La Joyeuse was *not* "just around the corner."

"Certainly not, Herbertson," I retorted with firmness, and, myself picking up a can of petrol—an inferior brand as it happened, but it was the only one within reach—I stalked out of the garage with all the dignity I could command in the circumstances. There must have been something in my manner which prevented them from following me. As I turned the corner I glanced back, and, to my surprise, saw the whole garage staff standing idly in the roadway, apparently watching me. I hope that they were observing what is the correct shade in egg-shell blue for shirts and collars, but even if they do, they will spoil it with something unsuitable, for the ideas of color of the people of Llwll are of course crude in the extreme. As they disappeared from my view, I could have sworn I heard a laugh. Something crude I had no doubt. I put Herbertson and all his menials out of my mind.

For some time past I had been toying with an idea. I should be going very near the post office. It would be in-artistic to appear in Llwll twice—besides, so much time would be wasted that my aunt's suspicions would be aroused. Yes, my mind was made up. Slipping the precious petrol can into the hedge, I made my way to the post office. I might as well get my books while I was about it.

"Good afternoon, Mr. Edward." Old Hughes, the post-master, seemed unusually genial and pleased to see me. He, of course, left a small child to whom he was selling pepper-mints, for he combines shopkeeper with postmaster, and, wiping his sticky hands on a rather grubby apron, he limped to the other end of his shop. "You've come for this parcel of books of yours, I suppose, sir. Fortunate thing, sir, we know

something of your habits, or we'd have sent them back to the
senders, and from what Miss Powell says, that would have
upset you fairly."

I quite refuse to believe that it is ever a fortunate thing that
other people should know something of one's habits, so I contented myself with a smile, rather a sickly one I am afraid.

Hughes took up a parcel—rather a larger one than I had
expected—with a cheerful smile. It was rather surprising
that both Hughes and Herbertson, whose manner to me was
generally distinctly surly, should apparently be so pleased to
see me. "Nice day for a walk, Mr. Edward," went on the
postmaster. "I'm afraid you will find these a bit heavy to
walk back with to Brynmawr. Of course Davies could bring
them tomorrow morning, if you wished, now that you have
told me they are for you, and I'm afraid, by the way, I'll have
to get you to sign some sort of receipt for them, but I'm told
you specially want them this afternoon, though I'm sure,
sir, that now you've seen how nice a day it is for walking,
you won't want to spend your time with books."

I let him rattle on, but this second reference to "walking"
must be checked. "Oh, I'm not walking," I said, "it very rarely
amuses me."

"Indeed, Mr. Edward," said Hughes, pushing his spectacles
up on to his sweaty forehead. "I understood you were, and I
didn't hear your car pull up."

"No, it's just round the corner, up the turning to Brynmawr," I answered, and with that I left him quickly, having
let him have as my final sentence the exact idea I wished him
to keep firmly in his mind. There is no denying it, brains
will tell.

It was with quite a singing heart I took the turning to
Brynmawr and retrieved my petrol can. I gave a glance up at
the back of the post office. It was a good thing that Hughes
was busy in his shop, and was besides too rheumatic to go
up and downstairs easily, or he might have seen me from his
windows. I looked up at them, and, to my horror, saw a distinct flicker of the hideous window curtain. This would never

do. I must not be seen. With the instinctive celerity of panic, I shot behind a tree from where I could watch, in all probability, without being seen. There was no further movement of the curtain. After a few minutes I resumed my dreary uphill walk.

But the incident had disturbed me. Herbertson's desire to go out of his way to take the petrol to the car, his and Hughes' geniality, Hughes' remark—what was it?—"I understood you were walking"—were all very suspicious. Now, why had he understood anything of the sort? Oh, yes, I remembered my aunt had telephoned to him about the books, and I believe had had the effrontery to say that I was going to walk down for them. Well, so I had, but I was not going to admit it to her or to old Hughes. If I had been prepared to do so, I should have fallen in with his suggestion that Davies should bring the books up next morning, and, having just given him his receipt, have left it at that. By the way, I had given him no receipt. Incredibly careless. Now couldn't I work something up about that? I must think.

But not just now. All these little incidents in Llwll, insignificant though they were, were nevertheless all a little odd. Supposing—a horrid thought—supposing my aunt had envisaged all this as likely, and was waiting on the road for my return! It was so possible, that, heavily encumbered as I was with the petrol in one hand and the heavy parcel of books in the other, without a second's delay I battered down a badly repaired gap in the hedge and got off the road into a field. There were some cattle there which pursued me a bit, but I got over the stile at the end of the pasture without having actually had to run.

Upon the happenings of the next hour I prefer not to dwell. I had to make my way by a circuitous route so as to enter the dingle a little way away from the road. I am not well acquainted—naturally—with the inside of the wood through which I had to go, and I must have lost my way slightly. Several times I climbed quite steep hills and, in the irritating manner of this country-side, was immediately obliged to descend them. Eventually, however, I safely reached La Joyeuse. With what pleasure I drove her up to the house, making as much noise as possible that my aunt should hear my triumphant return. I had of course to change, but I carefully put on a shirt of the same shade so that my aunt should not observe the fact. I had, however, some trouble in concealing a rather painful scratch from a bramble on my face. As a result I was a trifle late for tea.

"Well," said my aunt, barely troubling to finish a mouthful of cake, "enjoyed your walk?"

"My walk?" I flatter myself that I managed my eyebrows well.

"Yes, I see you've got another of those wretched novels."

"Yes." I refused to be drawn into a discussion on the relative merits of French and English literature, especially as my aunt really knows little of either.

"Then you walked down for them?" My aunt leant forward slightly in her rather upright chair, and stared at me intently, almost offensively.

I looked her straight in the face. "I left by car. I returned by car. Owing to the curious lack of petrol everywhere, I walked a few yards in Llwll. It delayed me slightly."

"Just a few yards, Edward?"

"Just a few yards, Aunt Mildred."

A silence fell. My aunt's face looked grim. She was taking her defeat in our little contest really rather to heart. I could almost find it possible to tell her that she had made me walk some way. It might comfort the old thing. But no, she might realize then that she had really won, and that would be intolerable.

"Very well, then, dear," suddenly said my aunt brightly, "you won't be too tired to help Evans and me put the wire-netting over the cherries. The birds will be at them soon, but we could leave it till tomorrow if you don't feel up to it."

Now it has unfortunately become an established custom that I assist in this unpleasant business each year. Apparently the netting cannot be put up by two people and apparently, too, my aunt has decided that I must assist, although other people could be found, I am sure. I did refuse one year, but my aunt merely refrained from putting up the netting. I like cherries while my aunt does not, and that year the birds got them all. But to choose this very afternoon for this annual performance, when I must admit that my whole body craved for rest, when my interrupted siesta, my aching feet, my weary arms, my tired muscles, and my scratched face, all loudly demanded a halt—to choose that moment was indeed hard.

However, my aunt must have no suspicion of this. Instantly I answered, "Feel up to it? I've never felt so fresh."

"You don't look it," said my aunt in a flat, significant voice, staring hard at the scratch on my face.

It was then that I realized what my feelings towards Miss Mildred Powell were. It was then that I mentally framed the sentence with which I have opened these notes!

It has been a great relief to write this typical incident down. I did it partly after dinner last night when the exhausting events of yesterday were finally over, and I finished it this morning. I think I shall go on keeping this rough sort of diary from time to time whenever I want to ease my mind. I see a new religious sect has got hold of the idea of "sharing" —only they apparently like sharing—or confessing—their sins with other people physically present, and I prefer sharing my troubles with these taciturn sheets of paper, which no one else will ever see.

4

The events of today have not been pleasant.

My aunt has been in a strange mood, and I never have known a woman who is so capable of conveying a sense of disquiet without saying anything. From breakfast-time onwards it has been clear that she has something on her mind. Several times she has been on the verge of saying something, and each time she has checked herself. At other times, too, she has seemed to be half inclined to laugh at me, which is a thing no man likes. Naturally enough, I have been wondering whether this attitude has anything to do with the little incident of the day before, and so as I have been putting down the notes I have written earlier on in this diary, I have written them rather fully and considered each point as I have done so. Is it possible that my aunt knows much more of my afternoon's adventures than I think she does? Can her action over that netting be entirely a question of spite?

That she is capable of being spiteful, I am sure; but can she know? I think not. So far as I can make out, there are only two things which may have made her even guess. One is the scratch on my face, to which, oddly enough, she has made no further reference, and the other is the length of time I had been away. But, after all, there are many possible reasons why I should be a little late for tea. One might be a natural desire to avoid her company after the *affaire* at lunch.

As I glance out of my window I can see my aunt on the lawn that slopes steeply from the French windows of the drawing-room to the meadow beyond the garden fence. Beyond the meadow, dotted here and there with old oaks under which Farmer Williams' cows are placidly sheltering from the afternoon heat, rises some miles off the crest of the Broad Mountain, a long hill, featureless and unworthy of the name mountain, but this afternoon quite pleasant to look at. Far away to my left the three peaks of the Golfas, the guardian pillars between England and Wales, are standing up dimly in the afternoon haze. One of my aunt's white pigeons is cooing sleepily, and only the faintest breeze stirs the leaves of the copper beech. For once I find myself liking the country-side, at peace with it. Only my aunt, weeding the rose-bed, strikes a restless note. My aunt would say, did she know of it, that the contentment of my mood was due to the exercise that I had taken yesterday. But then my aunt is capable of talking in public about my liver.

From across the meadow I see Williams coming and my aunt going to meet him. I know quite well that my aunt is going to complain of the presence in the home meadow of the cows—she will persist in a pedantic way in calling them young bullocks probably. With any luck she will work off her suppressed anger at her defeat on Williams. I can see from here that they are both distinctly angry.

It was at this moment that my aunt called me to her. It will be a great relief to put down her exact words while they are still fresh in my memory. I still boil with rage to think that any woman could be so rude, so treacherous, so capable of conspiring with subordinates, so malicious, so . . . I have broken my pen-nib writing it. I am not surprised.

When I reached her in the garden I found her almost trembling with rage. She has little self-control when these spasms of fury come on her. She began at once, totally ignoring the fact that Williams was present, "Edward, I never really like a liar."

I must admit it was weak of me, but I fear I must have blushed—largely of course for her. Stamping her clumsy garden boots on the lawn, she continued: "I'm glad you have the decency to blush. I put up yesterday with all your little silly lies. I didn't really mind your telling Herbertson and Hughes that your vulgar" (vulgar indeed!) "little car was just round the corner. You see I had laughed heartily when I saw you push it behind that bush in the dingle, and so did Herbertson and Hughes when they saw you start to walk back to here with that enormous parcel of books and the petrol can. You looked so funny dodging behind that tree, that they nearly gave themselves away. Where were they? Oh, looking out of the back of the post office of course.

"Yes, you may well look surprised. I don't suppose your feeble little make-believe story would have deceived either of them anyhow, but I want you to realize that when I say you are going to walk into Llwll, you *are* going to walk into Llwll. Of course Herbertson and Hughes were doing just what I told them, but as they both had a few scores to settle with your lordship, I thought they might as well have a good laugh also."

"Really, Aunt, I am surprised that you should demean yourself so." I was getting calmer, "It is unpleasant to think that these rustic people have been jeering at me, but if you are prepared to sink to the depths of plotting with the village postmaster to obtain it, well, really . . ." I was about to add that I hoped she was proud of herself, when she broke in vehemently.

"A man who is a hundred times more of a man than you, and, I regret to say, more of a gentleman."

"No doubt, my dear Aunt, your opinions are very interesting to Williams," I retorted. Had the woman no sense of the fitness of things?

"Mr. Williams is concerned in this matter too," was her surprising rejoinder.

"I really fail to see—"

"You would. That's just the point. Lies and liars, as I have said, I don't like, but I can understand your poor little attempts to keep up your precious dignity. When it comes, however, to a selfish disregard for other people's property, to ignorance of the first principles of how to behave in the country and a callous disregard for other people's convenience, or the safety of animals, then I will speak."

"Having, of course, been quite silent before, my dear Aunt." Light, however, was beginning to dawn on me. "Considering," I continued, "that Williams' cows chased me yesterday, I hardly see what you are driving at."

"There were at least two witnesses of what you did, young man." My aunt thrust her fiery face into mine, while Williams shifted from one shabbily gaitered leg to the other. "First of all, I myself was watching from the top of Yr Allt your progress up the road. You get an excellent view from there, and a lovely sight you looked by the way," went on my aunt, suddenly grinning broadly, "when you eventually struggled out of the Fron Wood and reached your precious car. Oh, a lovely sight, sweat pouring off you, bedraggled, scratched, your fat little body all panting, and your greasy fair hair quite rumpled. Oh dear, oh dear, what a lovely sight, and what a gorgeous, furtive, malevolent expression. And then the look on your face when I suggested putting the netting up over the cherries. I could have laughed aloud only that I was too angry with you." And with that my aunt positively put her hands on her hips and guffawed. I can use no other word.

There are moments when only silence can assert one's dignity. I started to stalk off to the house.

"Oh no," said my aunt, changing her mood at once, "you don't go yet. I haven't told you about the other witness, Owen Davies. He's had quite enough trouble with your precious books, so I thought it was only right he should have a chance of watching you carrying them back, especially after your remarks about him. He decided to go further up the hill, and so got an admirable view of your deliberate smashing down of Mr. Williams' fence."

"Really, what a bathos," I remarked. "All this to lead up to a badly and unnecessarily repaired gap in a fence!"

"Unnecessary indeed," suddenly snorted Williams, making his first contribution to the conversation.

"All right, Mr. Williams, let me go on my own way."

Williams deferred to my aunt at once. They all do round here. Somehow or other she seems to have a great influence over all of them.

"Not only," she continued, "did he see you break down the fence, but he saw Mr. Williams' mild cows wander slowly after you, as cows will when they want to be milked or just out of curiosity, and he saw you, you little coward" (my aunt's voice was really venomous) "deliberately stone them out of pure fright. Fortunately Owen Davies is a man, not a little cry baby who runs away from a cow. He repaired the

fence as best he could—do you realize that otherwise the
cattle might have strayed all over the road!—and he did
what he could for the cow you had injured. Now I can see
from your face that you don't realize what a little cad you
made of yourself, and so I'm going to try and bring it home
to you in one of the places where you will feel it—the pocket.
You're going to pay," said my aunt, thrusting her face towards
mine, and enumerating her points by wagging her fore-
finger in my face, "first, for the cost of repairing the fence
properly; secondly, for Owen Davies' time; thirdly, the
vet's bill; fourthly, for the loss of condition to the cattle;
fifthly . . ." My aunt paused and looked at Williams for
guidance.

"Milk," quoth that individual. I'm bound to admit he
looked a little ashamed of the profit he was going to make
out of my aunt's persecuting spirit.

"Yes, the milk," added my aunt, obviously not quite sure
how that came in.

"Wasted," said Williams monosyllabically.

"Yes, wasted," confirmed my aunt a little vaguely; "and
anything else I can think of," she added.

I turned to Williams. "One way and another it seems that
you are going to make a very good thing out of this." I faced
my aunt, and, mustering all my dignity, I said, "I shall be
happy"—a slight pause, and then with concentrated scorn—
"to pay."

With that I left them. For a second even my aunt was
silent. Then as a Parthian shot, she yelled across the lawn,
"Oh no, you won't be happy. But I shall see you do. I shall
stop it out of your allowance."

The unfortunate thing is that she will.

5

I must think the position over calmly. For I must admit that
some very strange ideas are coming into my head. Such a

mountain as is rising in my mind from the molehill of fetching a parcel.

Let me look the facts in the face. I hate living here. Yet why don't I leave this abominable and dreary place and my autocratic and domineering aunt at once, tomorrow, today, even?

The answer is simple. I can't, simply because my aunt holds the purse-strings. My father was unfortunate in his financial affairs. Indeed, I understand that it was worry over money matters which brought him and my mother to an early grave. There seems to be some mystery about it. At least I have never got my aunt or my grandmother, during her lifetime, to explain it to me. I notice that they change the subject or put me off when I try to find it out. Even the country folk and our neighbors, such as they are, never seem to mention my parents.

However that may be, my grandmother's will was curious. My aunt was made my sole guardian and trustee. Everything was to be hers for life, but out of it she was to make me an allowance, the size of which she was to determine, as long as I lived with her or in any place of which she approved. Should I leave her, she was under no moral obligation to assist me, and at no time was she under any legal obligation. She had absolute and entire discretion. On the other hand, she had apparently given a solemn promise to "look after me"—an attitude I resent, but must do my aunt the justice to say that I know she will keep any promise she has made. When she dies, Brynmawr, ironically enough, comes to me, and all the money. I shall sell the house and go and live in civilization. That is why I started my notes by saying that "my aunt lives just outside Llwll. That is exactly the trouble. Both ways."

I see, looking back, that I mentioned Surrey. But, of course, were I my own master, I should not live there. I only mean that it is more civilized as *country*. As a matter of fact I doubt if any part of Great Britain is really civilized. I shall ultimately dwell in Paris or perhaps Rome, if it were not for those frightful parres. The Riviera, Naples, and places like Ragusa and Istanbul, I shall visit occasionally, but certainly none of those raw British Colonies. I once met an Australian and the way he shook hands—

But I wander from my thread.

It is impossible then for me to live other than at Llwll, for my aunt refuses to give me an adequate allowance on which to live away from her—unless I am prepared to abandon all claim on her financially, for a while at least. I suppose, of course, I might take some degrading occupation, but I think anyone could see that that is impossible for me—quite, quite impossible. I have indeed tried my hand at a little modern verse, but there are too few cultivated souls to make this commercially successful, and indeed I am rather glad it is so.

So then at Llwll I must live while my aunt lives and insists on my staying there. And so tenacious is she of her promises, that I am afraid that nothing I can do will induce her to stop "looking after me," which she interprets as keeping me under her eye. If only, if only my aunt— No, I'm not going to think about *that* possibility. It makes my pen tremble, it makes the most frightful thoughts rise to my mind. I must put these pages away before I lose my calm. I will not think about it—I will not—I will not. That way lies—Oh, the rumors and suspicions I have of my father's death!

6

I have put aside this record for some days so that I might think things over quite calmly as I said I intended to do. Outwardly, relations with my aunt have resumed their normal standard, never at any time a really cordial one. Of course she has always got on my nerves. Her intensely masculine view of life and her complete disregard for appearances naturally would; but I have made a great effort not to let this affect me to any unusual extent. I have devoted a good deal of my time to So-so, my Pekingese. I find that his oriental face gives me a sense of philosophical calm. "What, after all," he seems to say, "does anything matter? You are, I suppose, the only friend I have in the world, and I would cheerfully sacrifice you if it helped my comfort in the least." Oh, admirable honesty and frank cynicism!

On the whole I think he is right. A spirit of true steel, even if it is incased in a "fat little body with greasy fair hair," and I should like to say that my hair tonic is *not* greasy —should be prepared always to face facts.

Very well then, let me face the facts. I meant what I wrote when I recorded that the trouble was that my aunt lived in Llwll. I should be very much happier if she were dead, and if I could see the way to do it safely, I have now been exasperated to such a pitch, that I would see to it that that desirable end was achieved, preferably painlessly. But alas! I cannot see the way.

However low an opinion one may have of the legal authorities of Cwm, one must see that if Miss Mildred Powell were to meet with an untimely end by obviously violent means, suspicion would be bound to fall on her only relation, the only person who would benefit financially by her death, and with whom she had recently been known to quarrel. And if, more-over, that person were the cause of her departure from this world, he would be automatically and inevitably in a position of great danger. Besides, I do not think honestly that however ingeniously I arranged matters, and however certain I was that I should ultimately be released, I should be capable of standing the long-drawn-out agony of suspicion, questioning, pressing interrogation, possibly even of trial.

The fact is quite clear. I am too obviously the person to be suspected to allow of any sudden end to my aunt, however detached from the matter I might apparently be, and however compact and certain an alibi I might have arranged to pro-vide. The question therefore cannot arise, and I will think of it no more.

I had written so much when I was interrupted by a curious incident. So-so has for a long time past carried on a feud

with my aunt's white pigeons. He has a strong, and to my
mind entirely reasonable, objection to their presence in the
house, and he never sees them in the garden but he pursues
them clamorously, though in vain, his legs being all too
short. My aunt, however, will induce them to eat out of her
hand and will encourage them to come in through the French
window, which she will fling open on the bitterest winter
day regardless of the rush of freezing cold air she is letting in.
Just now So-so was sleeping peacefully in the sun, the red-
brown of his coat toning in charmingly with the golden brown
of the carpet, and so still was he lying that one of the pigeons,
fluttering in all unasked through the window, not only failed
to see him, but walked straight into his comic little button
of a nose.

Naturally he snapped. Any dog would. I am not particularly
fond of the pigeons, but I wish So-so had not killed that one
in my room at that particular moment. For one thing, there
is a small, but quite definite, stain on the carpet. For another
thing, it was an accident too near to my thoughts. If only my
aunt would walk into the jaws of fate in some such way and
meet a similar accident! I must get Evans to bury the pigeon,
I suppose. Otherwise So-so will misbehave himself with it.
It had better be buried some way off or So-so will dig it
up again. It is all extremely tiresome.

7

It seems hardly credible, but even this trivial pigeon became a
bone of contention between my aunt and myself. Once more
the matter started at lunch; indeed, except at meals I generally
manage to avoid my aunt.

"Steak pie, dear?" said she, with an accent on the "dear"
which I can only call hypocritical; "not pigeon pie, I am
afraid. Your lap-dog only managed to catch a very old bird,
Evans tells me."

It would, I knew, be useless to argue with her and point

out how essentially unfair her assumptions were. Accordingly silence fell for some few minutes. My aunt turned her rather heavily built shoulders in order to repulse So-so, who was asking her in his charming way for a share of the pie. I always admire the spirit with which he tries to win my aunt's affections and attempts to get his tit-bits from the hardest source, instead of taking the easier course of appealing to me.

"A horrid little dog," remarked Aunt Mildred; "if he doesn't learn to behave soon, we shall have to get rid of him."

This was a bit too much for me. "I shall not allow that. Please remember that he is my dog."

"And it was my pigeon."

"It walked straight into him when he was asleep and began to tease him. Naturally the dog snapped."

"Yes, naturally, after his master has encouraged him to chase the pigeons whenever he sees them."

In my agitation I unfortunately allowed a piece of steak to go down the wrong way and was consequently quite unable to reply to this. Moreover, my aunt, under the impression that she was applying a restorative, leapt up and dealt me several blows on the back of so severe a nature that tears were almost brought into my eyes.

"In the future, my dear Edward," she continued, returning to her chair, "you will control him better. Or—I shall take action." An ominous phrase of hers which I had learned from an early age presaged something inevitable and extremely unpleasant. I shot a glance of scorn, and, it must be admitted, a little alarm at her ill-fitting and too youthful blue blouse. In her gray-green eyes was a look of intense conviction, and the nostrils of her large nose were quivering with determination.

"I shall look after So-so, poor dog, Aunt Mildred," I said, "even if no one else does." With that I gave him the choicest morsel on my plate. Unfortunately it was too hot for his delicate tongue, and he spat it out on the carpet and followed that by being instantly slightly sick.

"You don't do it very well," commented my aunt grimly,

"but you can make a start by clearing up the mess. You'll find a duster in the drawer of the cupboard in the hall."

I really do not see why my aunt should always have the last word.

By the time we had finished lunch it had started to rain. There is nothing more depressing in the world than this country-side in wet weather. The clouds collect so rapidly on the hills to the west of us that it is never safe to rely on the forecasts given in the papers or by wireless. One minute the sky is blue and the sun shining and you feel certain you are going to have a fine day; the next, down have come the clouds and the whole district is blotted out in a deep-gray mist of incredible dreariness, and with the clouds comes a cold, misty drizzle, which turns into a downpour, which lasts for hours, perhaps for days. As I look out of my window, I can see the meadow beyond the garden, but the cattle are gone, and there is nothing but sodden grass and dripping trees. Gone too is the Broad Mountain behind banks of clouds and the Golfas might be in another world. One feels isolated, cut off from all mankind, lost and surrounded beneath count-less miles of impenetrable gray, blanketing wetness. The wind whistles over the top of Yr Allt—my aunt could not today have sat there and jeered as she watched me toiling painfully up the road from Llwll—and tugs at the creeper on the side of Brynmawr. I can see little but the window-sill of my room, painted a hideous shade of pink, which always reminds one of that depressing substance, anchovy sauce. I did once remon-strate with my aunt as to this color, and received the crushing and irrelevant answer that it always had been painted that color.

Always had been! My aunt's great idea so far as decorating the house is concerned, both inside and out, seems to be that a thing is right because it is traditional. Except in my own room there is not a note of modernity anywhere. And as for my aunt's idea of color! I did try to explain to her once how deeply the surroundings, especially the color of one's sur-roundings, affect the texture of one's very soul. She only retorted by some very personal comments on a pullover I happened to be wearing. It was, perhaps, a trifle loud; crushed strawberry may be a little too bright for my fair complexion, but there was no need for her to say what she did.

And so her drawing-room remains unalterably the same. A carpet with a meaningless pattern, largely of olive yellow, very distressing, which she admits is not satisfactory but which she refuses to discard on the ground of economy; wallpaper—fancy, wallpaper!—covered with a meaningless pattern of roses and vine knots, which I believe was fashionable when that entirely deplorable man, William Morris, first started his curious theories on the "Home Beautiful"; chairs, either covered with ill-fitting chintz covers made locally, because poor Miss Somebody in Llwll must be given work, or standing nakedly bedizened with, of all things, red plush—dirty, worn red plush. I shudder whenever I go into the room.

Above the mantelpiece of white marble is an ornate gilt mirror, and in front of it stand incredible little pieces of pseudo-Dresden china, shepherds and shepherdesses, in glass cases, if you please! In the middle, incongruously, is a very plain traveling-clock in a shabby leather case. It has earned the place of honor because, forsooth, it keeps good time. As if time did not stand completely still at Brynmawr. I once ventured to point out this symbolical fact to my aunt, but she only took it literally.

"Not at all, dear. Time goes on here just as much as anywhere. As a matter of fact, cook is very punctual with her meals. It's you who are late," and then she broke off onto some uncalled-for remarks on my natural liking for my meals and preference for having them hot; criticism, criticism, always nagging criticism—and of me too!

Well, I must stop writing for the present. We are due to go and have tea and play bridge this afternoon with Dr. Spencer and his futile wife. They live about a mile on the other side of Llwll, and I do not fancy that the drive will be amusing. In fact I think I shall go and suggest to my aunt that we put them off.

8

Of course I wasted my time on that errand. I might have known that any suggestion, however sensible, would be turned down if it came from me.

"But, my dear, we promised the Spencers we would go." My aunt put down her knitting and stared at me with apparently genuine amazement. "You can't let people down like that."

"Really, Aunt Mildred, you are a martyr to your ideas of morality. I'm sure the Spencers don't really want to see us. No one would want to see anyone on this typically Welsh afternoon, I should imagine." With a wave of my hand, I indicated the excruciating weather. I find it a sure way of getting a rise out of my aunt, who finds it necessary to praise slavishly everything belonging to Wales, including even its appalling climate.

"You're not afraid of getting wet, are you?"

"I see nothing clever in getting wet, Aunt Mildred; but as a matter of fact there is no need to do so. I imagine that not even you propose to walk on such an afternoon. No, I merely think that it will be dull and boring, and surely one may occasionally accept an invitation when one can think of no reason for refusing at the moment, with every intention of getting out of it later."

"And how would you propose to do so?"

"Oh, ring up and make some excuse."

"Certainly not, Edward; I have no intention of telling any lies to gratify your passing whim. Besides, the Spencers are very charming people, and you wouldn't be alive if Dr. Spencer hadn't been a very able man."

This dragging in of an alleged benefit, many years old, the magnitude of which I beg leave to doubt, was simply maddening. My aunt's arguments are never relevant.

She continued to look at me severely. "I believe the real reason," she went on, "is that you are afraid of losing money if you cut against me. Well, I daresay you are a bit hard up with paying Williams, so if you like I'll carry you."

This was a challenge that could not be refused. "Certainly not," I said. "Even if luck has been against me, I am quite prepared to back my bridge against yours or against the Spencers', even if I do cut with you." My aunt ignored the implication. "Very well then. That's settled." She gathered up her knitting. "We'll start in five minutes. I'll have the car round by then. And, by the way, Edward, while we are there, try not to be rude." She shut the door before I had time to reply.

Normally when we go out we generally have some discussion as to which car we shall go in. My aunt maintains that no respectable woman should travel in a car with the seductive lines of La Joyeuse, and I—well, I hate to be seen in anything so out of date as my aunt's Morris. Besides, my aunt's idea of driving is, to say the least of it, terrifying. It often ends in our going separately. However, on this occasion I let her have her way. There was some truth in her comments on my financial affairs, crude though it was of her to have mentioned it, and the economy of petrol, trifling though it would be, was wise. Besides, by the arrangement she had proposed, she would have to go out into the wet to fetch the car. The best retort I could make would be to wait patiently by the front door.

My aunt took this somewhat amiss. She seemed to think that something would have been gained if I had gone out with her, though why I can't imagine. She was still murmuring something about manners and chivalry when we reached the Spencers'; she must have been deeply moved, for my aunt is not given to murmuring.

Naturally I was not giving her my whole attention. An idea was forming in my mind. Judging by the way my aunt drove, it seemed more than likely that sooner or later she would have a bad smash; now if only that accident could come soon! There are some quite dangerous places just outside the gates of Brynmawr where the ground falls away steeply from the side of the road to the bottom of the dingle. If a car were to go over the side, it would roll over and over and over right to the bottom. I found I could visualize the scene clearly. In fact I had difficulty in driving it out of my mind, so distinct in every detail was it. An accident to a careless driver, one who messed about for no obvious reason with the top of her float chamber, how suitable, what poetic justice! I had to exercise considerable will power to realize that I was confronted by Mrs. Spencer.

I suppose that this idea distracted my attention from my bridge. My thoughts would *not* concentrate on trifles such as trumps and sevens and eights. Besides, it surely is unnecessary to think at auction. Contract has not yet been heard of at Llwll. When it is, my aunt will merely say, "But we have *always* played auction," and apparently that will settle it.

As a matter of fact I think I wrong myself in what I have written. There was nothing amiss with my game. I do not know of any single case in which I did anything which was really wrong. It was simply that I had the most infernal luck. Of course my aunt does not know the difference between bad luck and bad play. She merely goes by results. If a finesse fails, or a jack is unexpectedly guarded, my aunt will always invent some reason to blame me for not seeing the probability, or, as she will say, the extreme likelihood or even certainty, of that happening. And I did have one of those afternoons when not a single finesse would go right. My aunt, on the other hand, always played in the way which the mathematical probabilities clearly showed was wrong, as I would have demonstrated to her if she had condescended to listen, and by some amazing freak the right way of playing the hand always led to disaster, whereas the wrong way gave my aunt triumph after triumph.

Dr. Spencer, too, is an infuriating person to play bridge with. He is one long question mark. "Whose deal is it? Oh, your deal. Ought I to cut? Is it my call? Oh, you dealt, did you, what did you say?" The unfortunate dealer indicates that he has said "one spade," and is tempted to add, "three times." "Oh, yes, one spade, you did say spade, didn't you? Yes, thank you so much. Then I'll say no bid." And so he goes on throughout the hand, during which he always asks (*a*) what the contract is, (*b*) what are trumps, (*c*) whose lead it is, whenever it is his, besides on an average ten more questions of varying kinds of futility. The only time he does not ask a question is when his partner does not follow to a suit; as a result of this remission he made me revoke twice. Naturally when he plays the hand, he usually forgets what he is trying to do, and frequently leads from the wrong hand with the attendant penalty. He let me down very badly.

It was not until the last rubber that I held any cards at all, and then, just as my luck was turning, Dr. Spencer must needs say, "Well, I'm glad you've had a consolation rubber, Edward. Not been doing much good today. However, it's all good experience."

Now, why because he mishandled (as I have no doubt he did) my youthful ailments, should he presume to talk to me like that? Good experience, indeed! I've forgotten more about bridge than he's ever known, and I don't go "four spades" on six to the queen with one king outside as my aunt does. If I did, I shouldn't find three aces and a singleton in dummy as she always does. Not very valuable experience that. Card sense and instinct indeed! What a claim for my aunt to make! She always does say that sort of thing to justify her more brazen performances. I shouldn't be surprised if old Spencer kicked her under the table. He's quite capable.

Of course auction is an out-of-date game, and contract, though modern, is really rather crude, like so many things American. Civilized people nowadays are playing the French version, plafond.

And so home to my aunt's idea of dinner, made worse by her patronizing attempt to refund what she had won from me. Menus at Brynmawr, like the furniture, are constructed on the principle of sticking to established traditions. No new dish, no delicate sauce, no flair is ever shown by cook. Just plain, solid, dull English food, good enough in its way, I must admit, but unvarying. However, I generally have a healthy appetite.

And so to bed, and to dream. To dream all night of a Morris car turning over and over, down the steep bank leading to the dingle.

"Edward," said my aunt this morning at breakfast, "you should not eat so much dinner. I heard you yelling in your sleep several times last night."

2: Brakes and Biscuits

For some time past now that particular spot on the road just outside Brynmawr has fascinated me.

The front gate of the house is some thirty or forty yards from the front door, before which is an open space of asphalt, useful but hardly ornamental. I think my aunt is aware of its lack of beauty, for on the left-hand side of this space as you come out is a border containing bulbs in spring, various flowers in the summer, and dahlias in the autumn on which my aunt lavishes even more than her usual considerable care, for she is devoted to her garden and even occasionally forces me into assistance in this pursuit, so tiring for the body and the intellect. Still I must admit the success of her efforts as to flowers and vegetables. Fruit eludes her as a rule, since the sun so seldom shines in this desolate spot.

As you stand by the front door then, to the left of the asphalt is her best border, to your front and rather to the right is a patch of lawn, which is a slight bone of contention, my aunt constantly bemoaning the fact that it is too small to play tennis on, while the ground slopes so steeply in all directions that it would be impossible to enlarge it without constructing a colossal embankment, which would be extremely unsightly. My aunt however would be quite prepared to erect such a monstrosity, but is fortunately restrained by expense. For myself I should like to use it as a croquet lawn, a form of exercise which I admire and which I understand is likely to become fashionable once more among modern people. There is an aesthetic grace in the

movements, a pleasant, simple symbolism in the impingement
of red on yellow and blue on black. Moreover, one can in-
dulge one's primitive passions by destroying completely one's
adversary's plans, and leaving him hopelessly and helplessly
wired from any reasonable possibility of success. What are
games for, except to release one's complexes by a little flavor-
ing of spite? My aunt however has some objection to croquet.
She implies that it is effeminate. Moreover, to her generation,
it is out of date. She cannot realize that there can be a revival
in games as well as fashions.

From the garage to the front gate there are two ways.
There is an extremely narrow passage by the side of the
house which enables cars to be brought to and from the
front door. There is also a way through the back-yard gate
on to the road which runs behind the border I have mentioned, but six feet or so below it. The narrow passage and
the wall behind the border are of recent date, having been
constructed by my aunt. They serve well enough for her
car and mine, but when my friend Innes who runs a Bentley
comes to stay with me it is almost impossible for him to get
around without damaging the wings of his car. Naturally my
aunt refuses to allow that her construction of this passage was
inadequately considered, and blames the innocent Innes for
having so large a car. Characteristically she takes no notice
of the damage to his Bentley but refers to Innes whenever he
is mentioned as "your friend who scratched the paint off the
side of the house." She will usually accompany this by turning her eyes to anyone who is standing near, or to heaven if
no one is, and murmuring, "Such a careless driver." In this
way she hopes to escape from the consequence of her own
lack of foresight!

From the front gate the road to Llwll bears slightly to the
right, and then turns quite sharply to the right, having the
meadow in which Farmer Williams puts his cows on the
right, and the steep bank of the dingle on the left. Then it
swerves sharply to the left and continues its descent to the

little stone bridge at the bottom over the Brynmawr brook.

I must admit that the bridge over the stream is often a charming spot. The banks of the dingle, covered with primroses in early spring, and later with bluebells and wild anemones, have always a certain fascination for me, and the little brook is always pleasantly chattering. In the autumn there are as good blackberries there as anywhere else, and I am delighted when my aunt gathers them and will even help her, though I prefer collecting the succulent mushrooms that abound in the grass at the bottom.

It was there I was sitting this morning, thinking, when I was recalled to a sense of my present surroundings by my aunt's voice and the barking of dogs. My aunt, I should say, has two mongrel fox terriers. At the time when she acquired them she had just been reading some absurd comic history of England, full, I gather, of elementary humor of the schoolboy variety. In this, two silly words coined by the author had fascinated her.

I remember her staring at these uninteresting but innocent white quadrupeds with black markings and saying suddenly:

"I shall call them Athelthral and Thruthelthrolth."

I recoiled in horror. I knew my aunt's sense of humor. She was quite capable of standing in the public street of Llwll or Abercwm or even Shrewsbury, and calling out, "Athelthrolth, Thruthelthral, Thruthelathelthrothel, Althelthrothelthruth," and getting redder and redder in the face until bursts of primitive laughter compelled her to stop, while the bystanders must inevitably think her crazy. I only hoped that I should never be compelled to stand by and listen.

I made a desperate attempt to avoid such a disaster.

"Why not call that one Spot?" I suggested.

"Why?" said my aunt.

"Well, he's got a black spot on his—er—" I paused delicately.

"On his rump," said my aunt coarsely. "I think"—she stared hard and pointedly at my forehead where it chanced there

was a slight gathering—I am rather subject to these minor
unpleasantnesses, but there is no need to call attention to
them—"I think I shall call *you* Spot," and she did for some
days, until fortunately even she got tired of the alleged
witticism.

However, Athelthral and Thruthelthrolth her dogs remained, though fortunately convenience has shortened them
to Athel and Thruthel, to which they answer. Unfortunately,
however, they have a dislike, heartily reciprocated, for So-so,
of whom they are jealous because he is allowed in the house
and they are not. It was the noise of their ill-bred attack
which roused me from my reverie. It is curious how animals
take after their owners.

My aunt's voice broke in. "Do stop dreaming and pick up
your beastly pet, unless you want Athel to kill him. He's a
very good ratter. I can't hold Thruthel back much longer
either," and indeed the dog was straining to get at my poor
So-so.

With one quick motion I kicked away the barking Athel
and swept So-so, still yapping defiance courageously, into my
arms.

"And another time don't you dare to kick my dog—or
anyone else's dog." My aunt glared at me. "Do you understand?"

I half turned my back on her and looked up the steep bank
of the dingle. My mind was made up.

"I see. I am to allow you and your curs to kill my dog
without stirring a muscle in self-defence. No, my dear
Aunt. No."

There was a contest of wills for some few moments as
we glared into each other's eyes. Very much, I have no doubt,
could have been read in both. I was the first to turn away and
saunter up the dingle. My aunt continued up the road, and
afterwards I slowly followed her. It is a fatiguing hill, and
I had no desire to be passed on the way up by my aunt,
who always runs rather than walks; nor had I any intention
of hurrying. But my mind was made up.

2

I think it was really made up some time ago; but perhaps it was true to say that that moment was decisive. I might have gone back on my decision before then, but now it is irrevocably fixed.

But it is all very well to make up your mind that somehow or another your aunt shall pay the penalty of her bad driving and shall come crashing down to that bridge where she has so insulted you, and in sight of the very bush where she has jeered and laughed at you, the slipperiness of her beloved road caused by the eternal rain of her idolatrously and senselessly loved Wales being perhaps a contributory cause: it is another thing to arrange for it to happen—especially when for the reasons I have already explained it is essential that no chance of suspicion shall fall on you.

I have been thinking over many ways, but there seems to be some difficulty in each case.

My first idea was that I should wait for a moonless night on which I knew my aunt was going to drive out, and then place some obstruction on the road. This would probably mean waiting some months, as at present it does not get dark until very late, and it would be no good arranging for her to run into it as she came up hill. She would not be going fast enough to be hurled over the bank.

Not that I am not prepared to wait provided the plan seems good enough; but I very much doubt if it is. In the first place the obstruction must appear natural, otherwise there will be inquiries, and it is very hard to block a road with anything sufficiently large to do the work required, sufficiently small not to be obvious yards before by the headlights of the car, and which might reasonably have come on the road by natural causes. A branch of a tree would be insufficient unless of fair size, and a trunk would be seen. Besides, how am I to supply it, unless I cut down one of the trees by the side of the road, the exertion of doing which would be prohibitive, besides the fact that one cannot do it unobserved, nor is it easy to make it look natural. I have examined all the trees, and none of them look in the least likely to fall, nor is there a telegraph pole conveniently placed.

There are, it is true, some very dark places on the road before it starts to go down hill where some heavy obstruction might be placed without being too visible, but they are all quite near the house, and my aunt always starts slowly, partly because her old engine prevents any other course, and partly because of the sharp corner on the road. Moreover, supposing that my obstruction is placed there, it is still possible that some other vehicle might run into it. It is unlikely, since Brynmawr is on the road to nowhere practically speaking, and behind the house the road turns into the veriest lane, little more than a cart track leading up to the heather and bracken that surround the Old Farm where Williams lives and his sheep graze. It would give me no compunction at all that my obstacle should hurt Williams when he returns drunk from the Llwll market, but his horse would probably stop before running into it, and drunk or sober, Williams would remove whatever was there, and then no obstacle of any kind could be replaced there for fear of causing questions to be asked.

Moreover I know of no natural obstacle that I could put there, nor an artificial one that I could remove immediately afterwards without leaving some trace of its having been there. The method seems to be uncertain (which is highly undesirable) and difficult to execute, and, what is worst of all, risky. Unless I can get some really good idea on the subject, I shall not try it.

I have been wondering if I could cause her car to catch fire while my aunt is sitting in it. It is very significant that in all my dreams (and they occur almost nightly now) it is a *blazing* car which is rolling down the side of the dingle. There have been cases reported in the papers where people have, or are said to have, got rid of some undesirable person and then burnt them while sitting in a car. It is, however, a very remarkable fact, that fire *does not seem to do its work properly*. Only too often I notice the body is not entirely burnt, and then these busybodies of police doctors come along and are able to make the most alarming and almost inconceivable deductions. I shall not therefore be so foolish as to attempt to burn my aunt's body. Besides, this method involves as a first step the actual physical killing of my aunt, and I do shrink with a natural and, I think, commendable squeamishness from that actual deed. Blood is so repellent.

In fact, the very thought is so disturbing that I had to stop writing and read a story of de Maupassant's to calm my nerves, before I could continue to write these notes. It may seem absurd, by the way, to write them at all, but I find that a frank discussion of the courses open is very beneficial to the intellect. After all, soldiers, I believe, though a stupid class of people, are encouraged to attempt to stimulate their brains into thinking by writing what they call an "appreciation."

But to resume. Is it then possible to arrange some contrivance so that the act of starting the car and driving off would start some electrical contrivance or time machine of some sort which should ultimately set fire to the car? The machine might be put as near as possible to the petrol tank, and it might be operated by a wire attached to the gear lever, so that the act of putting the car in gear would start the machine. There are great advantages in this method. The machine and the attendant wire and all possible fingerprints would be destroyed by the fire. It would be automatic, and it could very well occur at a time when I was nowhere near the spot.

Let me think of any possible disadvantages.

Well, firstly, my aunt might be quick enough to get out. I really don't know about that, but I should imagine that the effect of a spark on petrol confined in a close space would be a pretty well instantaneous explosion. I should like to experiment but there are obvious difficulties! And then the spark must, I suppose, be *in* the petrol tank, but yet I imagine if whatever gives it is beneath the petrol, there might, so to speak, be no spark. But then probably it would be possible to arrange that it was above the top of the petrol. I should have to wait my opportunity when the tank was not quite full, a condition that must frequently occur.

Yes, there is much to be said for this. And a little revenge by means of petrol would be suitable. Unfortunately, how-ever, there is one rather serious drawback. I have not the slightest idea of how to make such a machine, and I can hardly ask! Still, it must be possible to find out. I will keep the idea in mind. It has very great possibilities.

Promising though this is, I will not abandon considering all other ways. A very obvious idea, suggested by my aunt's driving, is to tamper with the steering. Nothing is easier than a little weakening of the steering rod, but nothing is more certain than that if there is one place where steering has necessarily to be careful it is when leaving the garage of Brynmawr and going down to the front gate, whether you go by the narrow passage to the front door, or by the yard gate and the road. If there was anything wrong with the steering, it is almost certain that my aunt would find it out *before* she went down the hill to the brook.

But supposing there was nothing wrong when she started, but that any sudden jerk to her steering wheel would cause a break in the steering rod, and supposing that I arranged that there should be some sudden need for her to swerve? Supposing, for instance, that I arranged that So-so should run across the road just in front of her in the dark patch where the drive swings to the right? She would not, I be-lieve, be so callous as deliberately to run over my poor Peke, and so she would try to go to the left (there is a bank on the right), and to come sharply back to the right, but then, smash!—and on would go the car, *not* to the right, but straight down the bank in front.

Now is there no flaw in that? Yes. Supposing she puts on her brakes hard. She will be going slowly at the time, and she will stop before she reaches the drop, and then there might be no smash-up of the car and the steering gear might be examined, and then who knows what might happen? But there is an obvious means of avoiding this. *Her brakes must not work.*

That's it, the steering rod nearly broken and the brakes out of action. One hole in the master cylinder and the piston inside will not send the brake fluid along the pipes to any of the brakes on each of the wheels, and the cam will not push out the shoes onto the brake drum, and down will go Auntie and Morris and all! In fact it's simpler than that: I needn't puncture the master cylinder—which might be noticed—I need only remove a nut so that the brake fluid escapes through the joints in the oil pipes and the trick is done. And who is to say that the nut did not work loose, the steering gear have a flaw, quite naturally? Herbertson perhaps should have noticed it last time he overhauled the car, but, with care, I can make the point that Herbertson is very careless in his repair work and quite untrustworthy, so careless that I never entrust my car to him. A further advantage.

I will think it over with the greatest care, but I think that plan should be satisfactory.

3

I have been reconnoitring the ground. Really my metaphors are becoming very military! Old Spencer has a son, an unpleasant, hearty sort of fellow, all loud bounce and hand-shaking, who has the most extraordinary attachment for that curious and depressing anachronism, the Territorial Army (after all, if war is abolished, why not be logical, I say, and abolish soldiers too? I have never met a really desirable one). Anyhow, it is from him that I suppose I have picked up this silly phrase. He never can see you looking at anything or finding out at, say, the County Ball, where the Supper Room is, without saying, "Reconnoitring? Time spent in reconnaiscanoe is rarely wasted, or is it 'really wasted'?" and with that feeble joke — apparently embodying a quotation from one of his foolish text-books—he will drop the owlish expression he considers good acting and laugh uproariously. He has no restraints, no real self-control. Only soldiers and schoolboys need text-books with such platitudinous maxims.

The point of my reconnaissance, however, is not so much, as young Spencer would say, the lie of the ground as the use of cover. In plain English I have been looking to see exactly where and how So-so is to be let loose to cause the necessary alarum. Moreover he must be rehearsed in his part; otherwise, nervous little darling that he is, he might refuse to cross the road with the car coming or run back to me, and I think it is advisable, just in case the plan is not entirely successful, that I should be neither seen nor heard, like a good little boy.

Now it is essential that the swerve and the crash shall take place just on the curve of the road; otherwise my aunt will merely proceed straight down the road, and that is of no interest to me. She must go right on over the edge and down into the dingle, and there must not even be a tree to stop her course until the car has gathered a really adequate momentum. Of course the sides of the dingle are nowhere quite free of trees, but if she goes over where I intend her to there will not be obstruction for some time, for a sufficient time for my purpose. If only one could explain it to her and mark out the spot with white lines on the ground!

However, that being impossible, it is clear that So-so must cross the road at a particular point (which I *have* marked with a stone), just about when the Morris is between the second and third trees from the front gate. Now the question is, how to induce him to do so, and where shall I be at the moment?

I have given this a good deal of thought. In the first place it is impossible for me to stand on the other side of the dingle and call So-so. He wouldn't stay there when I went away. Nor have I any intention of being on the bank of the dingle near the road. It would indeed be ironic if my aunt's car ran over me! No, I must be close so as to control So-so, and I must be hidden on the right-hand side of the road, that is to say behind the hedge that divides Farmer Williams' meadow from the road. On the left of the road, the dingle side, there is of course no hedge or fence—a fact which I know so well that I ought to have stated it before if I had considered anyone reading these notes. Behind this hedge then, I must be concealed, or perhaps, better still, behind the tree a yard or two into the field while So-so waits on the edge of the road, ready to rush across when I give him the signal, and that suggests to me the way to send him across —how this business of writing does help one's thoughts!

I have never favored teaching So-so tricks. The process is fatiguing, and the obstinacy of So-so really remarkable, but there is a particular form of sweet biscuit for which he will do anything. They are quite easy to come by, as there are always some in the dining-room, being home-made. From my earliest youth I have never known them called anything else than "Brynmawr crinkly biscuits"; they are made, I suppose, of flour and butter mostly, with sugar, and emerge as rugged little fingers of short-bread nature—very attractive. The scheme then will be to train So-so that one of these is to be found on the left-hand side of the road, and that he will be held on the right-hand side until I call out "Paid for," and let him free of the string round his collar by which I shall hold him. I can start by placing the biscuit so that he sees me do it, and taking him only just to the other side of the road before I let him go. Gradually I can extend the distance, so that he starts behind the hedge, and then get him used to my being behind the tree. Finally he must recognize the plan and be anxious to dash for the biscuit even if he has not seen me put it there. Fortunately So-so does not bark when he is under the influence of a really strong emotion, such as greed!

There was a slightly disturbing incident this morning. Acting on the principle that there is no point in wasting time, I had no sooner finished the words above than I went down to the dining-room to get some crinkly biscuits, So-so trotting happily at my heels, for the little wretch is well aware where his favorite dainty is kept. As it happened there were not a great many in the box, and after I had eaten a few myself I found that only seven or eight were left. Feeling that my time would be wasted if I conducted a rehearsal of less than eight performances, I naturally took the lot.

No sooner had I started for the drive than I heard my aunt's voice: "Edward, Ed-ward." I did not want to have her searching for me while I was teaching So-so his little trick, so, wisely, I went back to see what was the matter.

"Yes, Aunt," I called from the front door.

"Didn't you have any breakfast this morning?" came my aunt's voice from the dining-room.

"Yes, Aunt, very early."

"Nonsense, you were late as usual," my aunt could not resist the dig; "but, though I cannot say that I noticed it, you must have eaten nothing," and with that she clumped out of the dining-room brandishing the empty biscuit tin in my face.

"I did eat one or two, I think. I hope you don't grudge them to me?" Two can play at insinuation!

"One or two! Three-quarters of a tinful. I happen to know because I looked after breakfast to see if the tin wanted re-filling, and now, when I want one, it's empty. It seems that *you* grudge *me* any!" My aunt slammed the tin to and started to go off to the kitchen to see, I was glad to notice, that it was refilled. "In future I shall only put them out in small quantities. These rich biscuits are not good for you, Edward, when you eat pounds at a time. No wonder you get boils."

Now setting aside the injustice of her remarks, and they would have been unfair even if I had eaten all the biscuits instead of only some of them, this is a distinct nuisance. How am I to get an adequate supply with which to train So-so, for there is nothing else that I know of which is certain to attract his capricious little soul, which can be relied on to draw him across the road, even if there is a car coming along it. Well, somehow, they must be got. I am more than ever determined on *that*. I can take a few every day and reserve them entirely for So-so, though it will be hard to abandon them myself altogether, for So-so's taste is very sound—they are excellent biscuits. But perhaps a better way, and one which will avoid this self-denial, will be to persuade Mary, the parlor-maid, to bring me some occasionally direct from the larder. With a little cajoling I can generally persuade her to do what I want, tiresome female though she is. It will be a distasteful business, but in the cause of art, one must be prepared to make sacrifices. And I intend that my conduct, till this matter is over, shall be thoroughly artistic.

4

And indeed it is necessary that it should be so. Today I nearly made a slip. I have been now occasionally managing to conduct rehearsals for So-so. He really is extraordinarily intelligent, and I have now got him to the stage when he will sit for as long as I like, his brown body quivering with excitement, his little black tongue licking his jaws in anticipation; but, bless him, uttering no sound, ready for the moment when the string slips out from round his collar and he is free to dash for the much-wanted biscuit.

I have been training him to restrain himself for longer and longer periods, since I may have to wait some time for my aunt when the day comes that I put my plan into execution —it may perhaps be advisable that I should leave the house well before my aunt on that day, for I never forget that there must be no shadow of suspicion in my direction. So-so, then, is learning restraint. Once only has he broken through the discipline, and that was when Athel, wandering round by himself, hunting, I suppose, slipped up unseen by me, but noticed by So-so, and secured the biscuit. Then poor So-so made a dreadful scene, and really I can't blame him. He almost bit me in his frantic desire to prevent the theft of his property, by one, too, who was probably incapable of appreciating it.

Today, however, I was a bit careless. I had made So-so wait a very long while, so long indeed, that my attention had wandered. Suddenly I heard a footstep on the road, and in my surprise foolishly let go of the string that held So-so. In a second the brave little fellow had shot through the hedge and across the road almost under Farmer Williams' boots!

"Indeed to goodness," I heard him mutter, "and where would you have come from? And if you come here, where is your master?" His voice went up at the end in that ugly Welsh lilt and I could guess that he was looking round, searching for me; for Williams, a true Welshman, is incredibly curious.

At any moment now, I knew, So-so might finish the biscuit and, by returning to me, give me away. Quick as thought I crouched down behind the tree and turned over onto my back. Then I gave a very realistic snore.

"Oh, indeed," I heard Williams mutter, "so Mr. Edward is there. Indeed I would have thought he could have found better ways to pass the morning." I heard him turn from the hedge and try to make friends with So-so. "Look you here, you wee devil, you must not run so under my feet. Another time I might hurt you and though, to speak truth, I do not like you, I would not do that. Indeed I would not."

At this moment he must have leant down to pat So-so who naturally took it as an attempt to snatch part of his precious biscuit from his mouth, for I heard Williams continue:

"And what then would this be? A biscuit, indeed? And how would you find biscuits in the grass? And if then your master sleeps so soundly, he could not throw them for you. Indeed then he must have thrown you the biscuit just before I came up the side of the dingle and got on the road, and then he must have taken to sleep in one minute—or less. Indeed to goodness!" Williams paused. "But look you, I would not steal your biscuit, and it may be soon your master will forget that he and I had words about cows and about fences, and so I will wish you good day, and if you come to my house, you brown dog, you, I will say as I say to all my guests, 'Come in, small dog, and make yourself at home and take large mouthfuls.'"

So-so, I was glad to notice, scorned his clumsy attempts at a rapprochement—in fact he tried to accept the invitation to a "large mouthful" at once. For myself I continued to feign sleep. It was curious to notice that Williams really thought I should dislike meeting him, simply because my aunt had made a fool of herself about me in his presence. Of course I should never forgive him for his part in that incident, but I should not put myself to the trouble of altering my conduct to him because he had acted in an avaricious manner to me. He really was not worth bothering about, and I should have liked him to know it. It was perhaps unfortunate that he should have got a wrong impression from our little encounter, but perhaps that was better than that he should realize anything of what had been happening. I know a little, unfortunately, of these Welshmen. Their curiosity is insatiable, and he would have gone on asking question after question as to why I was giving So-so biscuits, why I should want to teach him tricks, why I should want to do it on the drive, and so on endlessly. It was not an altogether desirable explanation that he had invented for himself, but at least he would make it fit all the facts, and that would stop him from speculating, from dwelling too much on the subject and, after the event that was to come, from talking too much and causing pointless and undesirable conjectures. His pathetic and obvious attempt at reconciliation, however, I should ignore.

But as I walked back to lunch, keeping under the shade of the oak trees, I thought the matter over. I must be careful. I must see that neither my aunt nor anyone else saw me at that point of the road again. On the whole I thought I had better put my plan into execution pretty soon. So-so was sufficiently rehearsed, and I did not think I could continue to coax Mary any more without being sick. Besides, the

strain was beginning to tell on my health. I am sleeping
badly.

Indeed, I gather that this is beginning to show in my looks,
for my aunt commented on it at lunch. She seemed concerned
about me, but I am bound to say that sympathy loses its
kindliness when it chiefly consists in referring to the pastiness
of your face.

This afternoon I spent, while my aunt picked the currants,
nominally in overhauling La Joyeuse. My aunt asks me so
often exactly what I am doing that I think it advisable always
to have a ready explanation. Not, to be fair, that she is really
inquisitive or suspicious, and certainly not because she is
interested in what I do. It is simply her only idea of small
talk. I was therefore in a position, in case she asked, to talk
easily and naturally, about La Joyeuse's carburetor—a line
of conversation which I knew would quickly bore her. Actually, of course, I was examining her Morris more than my own
car.

The steering gear will be an easy job. It is, as a matter of
fact, none too good now. Indeed, if I leave it much longer
my aunt may notice the flaw in it herself and have it seen
to, which would be awkward. There is, however, a hitch
about the brakes.

I had thought that all cars were fitted with the type of
hydraulic brakes I have described, although a few models
have a metal rod forming a brake pedal to the wheels. My
aunt's Morris, however, is so antediluvian (I really think that
Noah must have had it on board the ark) that it is fitted with
a wire cable which operates the brakes.

There is only one thing to do with this. I shall have to cut
through eight of the ten strands and rely on the jerk breaking
the other two. It is not so sure as if I could put the master
cylinder out of action, and I shall have to be very careful in
my cutting through of the strands. They must be frayed, not
sharply cut, for it is possible they might be inspected afterwards. With luck, however, the car will be smashed up too
completely for that to be done. Anyhow, the cutting must

be done gradually, for the cut must not look new for each strand. I started this afternoon very cautiously and artistically. Much can be put down to the indifferent surface of the by-roads of Cwm.

5

I must spend the morning writing. It will help to keep me cool, and a clear brain is needed, *for I have definitely fixed on this afternoon.* If I describe what happened this morning it will help to keep my imagination from running away with me.

Breakfast can be a very charming meal. Breakfast at Brynmawr never is. In the first place a too slavish insistence on a particular hour is a mistake. A man should not be forced to rise before he has finished the sleep he really requires. Bathing and dressing should never be hurried, but at Brynmawr I am nearly always disturbed by my aunt calling: "Edward, Ed-ward," (how well I know the pause between the syllables in my name. It always means trouble) "are you getting up?"

Now the right answer is "No. I'm staying in bed this morning," but somehow I never have the courage to give it. At least I did once, and my aunt by dint of badgering and cross-questioning me got me to admit I was ill. Whereupon, instead of sympathy, tea and toast, and peace, she gave me a large dose of castor oil and no breakfast.

However, I answered as usual, "Yes, Aunt. *Just* coming. I —er—lost my collar-stud." Why do I make excuses? My aunt never believes me.

"All right, then. Hurry up. Breakfast is getting cold."

"Can't it be kept hot?"

My aunt ignored this palpable hit. I know quite well that she deliberately lets it grow cold. I gave her a breakfast heater last year as a Christmas present, but she refuses to use it.

"I thought you hadn't heard the gong."

This, I might say, is one of my aunt's unvarying remarks. She knows perfectly well that no one can fail to hear that frightful instrument which no decent household has; Mary, by her special direction, beats it till I hope the brass will burst. But she also knows quite well that the stupidity of the pretense that that is her reason for calling to me has a curiously ruffling effect on my nerves.

I ought to have completed in my own time the business of dressing, but somehow or other, as usual, I allowed my aunt's action to influence me and scurried through the rest of the process without giving that attention to the question of whether my tie and socks really matched that I should have liked. At any moment my aunt might call again, and that I felt I couldn't bear.

With a feeling that something had been forgotten, I flew down the stairs, only after all about twenty-five minutes late. What a fuss about a trivial matter! I felt almost virtuous at my punctuality.

My aunt surveyed me coldly. "Well, I'm glad you had the grace to hurry. You can brush your hair afterwards." She poured out my tea and sat with the air of a martyr to watch me finish my meal. Now I am quite capable of passing myself the marmalade and giving myself my own second cup of tea —I prefer coffee anyhow—but I can never persuade my aunt to leave me in peace. Whether it is that she wants to make me hurry, whether she likes to rub in the fact that I am causing her a (largely imaginary) piece of inconvenience, or whether it is simply a desire to make me feel uncomfortable I do not know, but she does it regularly, heaving deep sighs at intervals and finally invariably saying, "Finished, dear?" and making for the kitchen with a great show of activity.

Of course breakfast should be eaten slowly and the pictures of one of the illustrated morning papers glanced at casually, but no paper reaches Llwll until lunch time, and my aunt reads nothing but the *Daily Telegraph.* I can't think why. Accordingly my options were to eat my lukewarm scrambled eggs and hardening toast in silence, or talk to my aunt. Thank heavens that if all goes well this afternoon I shall never have to endure such a meal again.

At first the silence was icy—so icy that I decided to break it.

"And what are you doing today, Aunt Mildred?" Not that at that moment my aunt's movements interested me much— of course I should be glad to know when she was out of the way so as to keep So-so fully rehearsed—but otherwise I was not really thinking much. One must, however, say something.

"Household duties in the morning, dear. There's the washing to do today, and that will take all that is *left* of the morning." (Brute.) "And this afternoon, of course, my hospital meeting."

"Hospital? Oh, that committee you're on. Really this toast isn't fit to eat. When's that?"

"Four o'clock. Really, dear, that's your *own* fault. It *was* excellent. Why so interested all of a sudden in the hospital, dear?"

"Oh, I just wondered. It's burnt anyhow."

My aunt eyed me grimly. She hates any criticism of her beloved cook, and I am bound to say that it is seldom that there is any need. Still, I don't think she is the paragon my aunt pretends she is. As I think I have said before, she has no imagination, no finesse.

"I suppose," she—my aunt, not the cook—said suddenly, "you want to know when I am out of the way."

This was so perfectly true that I started and spilt some very hot tea on my gray flannel trousers. It was painful, but that passed off; the stain, I am afraid, will not. However, let that be. My aunt's voice continued:

"Understand once and for all I will not have it. Mary's a very good girl and, besides being an excellent maid, is a daughter of Hughes of the post office, and I will have no unpleasantness for her under my roof."

"What on earth are you talking about?" I really was surprised.

My aunt looked me straight in the face. "The way you've been pestering Mary. I can tell you your attentions are un-wanted, and even if they were, I wouldn't allow it."

I tipped my chair back, which always annoys my aunt, and taking a cigarette from my lacquered green case, fairly laughed in her face.

"Attentions?" I trilled.

"Can you deny that you've been doing your best to fasci-nate Mary for the last ten days, ogling her and trying to make little secrets and assignations all day long. Why, I've seen you at it under my very eyes. And don't tip that chair up, you'll break the legs."

This must be stopped. I *am* very fond of Mary, and life would be very dull at Brynmawr without her. I forgot for the moment what has hardly ever left my mind recently, that I am not going to live at Brynmawr much longer.

"Really, my dear aunt, and what a mountain out of a mole-hill. Perhaps I had better explain. Won't you have a cig-arette?"

"You know I never smoke your scented horrors, Edward."

She went to the mantelpiece and got herself a Gold Flake. My aunt never uses a cigarette-case. It always makes me blush to see her produce a crumpled yellow packet and shamelessly offer it to other people. I paused while she struck a match on the sole of her shoe—another ungenteel habit of hers.

"Well, explain away," she added.

"It's an entire misunderstanding of course. You may re-member a few days ago that you saw fit to dole out the sweet biscuits in small and niggardly rations. I have no doubt that the ration was really adequate, had I been content to submit to the arrangement; but one has one's pride, so I thought, to put it shortly, that the simplest way was to arrange that Mary got some for me. It was an amusing little comedy, and I have no doubt we have smiled over it. I suppose that is what you unpleasantly refer to as 'ogling.'" She was hardly likely to guess what I wanted the biscuits for!

My aunt let out a puff of smoke right into my face. "Ingenious, Edward. Quite ingenious. And no doubt there is some foundation of truth in it, or you would not have thought of it so quickly. In fact I know there is. I naturally know all about the extra biscuits, but that was only the cover for your nastiness, the excuse in case you were questioned. It wasn't the real reason for your behaviour, I know perfectly well. In future that behaviour will stop, or—" and she fixed me with that stony glare and produced the phrase that always seems to paralyze me—"or, I shall *take action.* Meanwhile, in order that even the excuse may not exist, I shall give orders to Cook this morning that no more of those biscuits are to be made for the present. I shall take what she has made down to the hospital this afternoon, and as for those in the tin"—she walked across the room, and calling to her beastly pigeons, crumbled them up in pieces and scattered them outside the dining-room window.

There was a fine rumpus outside as Athel and Thruthel dashed up too, and drove the pigeons off, while poor little So-so, scenting perhaps his favorite food, but ignorant that it was possibly the last, came as fast as his short legs would carry him, only to be scared away like the pigeons by those ill-bred fox terriers. I caught him up in my arms. "Never mind, So-so," I whispered into his silky ear, "I've got two more hidden upstairs and you shall have one this afternoon shortly before four, and tomorrow, well, perhaps Cook will receive different orders tomorrow."

A liaison with Mary indeed! And even if I have flirted, ever so mildly, with her, what business is it of my aunt's? Really, she is too Victorian. All this business is intolerable. This morning I shall cut the brake-cable and this afternoon the Gordian knot. By scattering those biscuits on the ground, my aunt herself has precipitated matters. With only two biscuits left I must act before So-so forgets his part, or wait indefinitely till my aunt changes her orders to Cook. It must, then, be this afternoon before those biscuits are stale—I would not like to reward So-so with a stale one—and before

my aunt finds out that I have these precious two, and throws
them away, which really might happen when next my room
is turned out.

6

It has been terrible, perfectly terrible. I must put it all down,
every moment of it, just as it was all presented to me.

Lunch was grim. For various reasons no one was quite
normal. Naturally enough I was not entirely self-possessed.
Considering what I had to do that afternoon I should hardly
have been human if I had been. Even at that last moment
I found my resolution wavering. That my aunt deserved fully
all she was going to get, I was as fully convinced as ever, but
was there no other way round it? Couldn't she be persuaded
to let me go away and live my own life? After all, I had
never asked her. I half made up my mind to give her one last
chance. So far my eyes had been fixed firmly on my plate;
I lifted my head with a view to giving her that possibility
of reprieve directly Mary left the room. As bad luck would
have it, my eyes caught hers instead of my aunt's, and what
must the silly girl do but blush. Apparently she, too, was not
entirely self-possessed. Remembering my aunt's insults and
innuendoes of the morning, I felt a flood of color come across
my face. Significantly my aunt looked at me, and then at her
retreating form. That look did much to steel my nerves.

After all, perhaps it was *dangerous* to give her a last
chance? Supposing inquiries started, was it wise that our last
conversation should be a passionate appeal by me for freedom, for escape from the endless nagging, nagging, nagging
to which I was subjected day in and day out? Of course no
one would know what topic we had discussed when we were
alone, but such a theme once started would not be finished
in a minute, and my aunt, who was capable of such remarks
as she had made in the presence of Williams, might not be
restrained by the return of Mary with the pudding. A scat-

tered sentence at least, probably sounding all the worse by being torn from its context, would certainly reach Mary, and after what had happened I was no longer sure that I could trust that girl. They say that everyone who contemplates doing what I was going to do, makes one slip. I felt that to make such an appeal would be that slip. No, I must be firm, ruthless, resolute.

I turned my mind, thus made resolute, to my pudding. The spoon with which I was eating it crumpled in my hand. In silence my aunt seized it and straightened it.

"The Powells, my dear Edward," she said, "have lived at Brynmawr since 1658. That spoon was over a hundred years old." She peered over the mark on the silver. "Yes, over a hundred. We have always held our head high in the country. It's a pity to break old spoons in a fit of temper because you can't have your own way in everything. It's a pity to depart from old traditions. No cheese, thank you."

It was so like my aunt to spoil her dignity by such a conclusion. It was so like my aunt to seize the pretext of an accident to deliver a sermon. And what a sermon! Ever this harping on the merit of perpetuity, on absence of change.

Still there was something rather fine about it. Now that she had come to the last few hours of her life I could not help a little sentiment creeping in. Should I, after all, relent? I have really a very kind, unselfish, and forgiving nature. I stole quietly away to a disused attic to think. Kindly feelings were stealing over me. Below, I heard my aunt going to my room. I congratulated myself, prematurely, on my wisdom in selecting the attic.

"Edward, Ed-ward," came my aunt's voice. "Edward. Damn the boy. I never can find him when I want him. Edward." A pause followed, during which I heard my aunt move across the hall. This was followed, to my horror, by a violent beating on the gong. This was more than I could bear. I emerged wearily.

"Yes, Aunt."

"Going deaf, dear?"

"Rapidly—that gong."

My aunt's glance suddenly turned from the vaguely ag-
grieved to the actively suspicious. "What on earth are you
doing up there?"

Had she but known it, this was a very difficult question to
answer, and one, moreover, it would have been better if she
had not asked. As it was I found a reply difficult. "I—er—was
thinking."

"In the attic? Thinking? Why not in your own room? Why
on earth go up to the maid's part of the house? Really, Edward, if I thought—"

This was more than I could stand. I faced her squarely.

"Aunt Mildred, you have a filthy mind."

For once in her life my aunt was so taken aback that I had
the last word. I was able to leave her gasping, her large
mouth opening and shutting feebly, and showing her badly
stopped teeth in great and revolting detail. With So-so at my
heels I strode from the house. Quickly I made my way round
to the garage, though by a circuitous route. In a few seconds
I had perfected the last details of my plan. Then I walked
off a little way up Yr Allt, the hill behind the house on the
other side to the drive. There I produced a book from my
pocket and ostentatiously sat down to read in full view of the
house.

Presently I saw my aunt come out into the garden. She
apparently felt the need to work off steam, for she fell to
work on clearing away the vines of some early peas which
were over. Pull, tug, up came the old plants; jerk, and the
sticks on which they were grown were pulled up; heave, and
they were stacked neatly at the end of the garden for future
use. From where I was I could see her hurrying to and fro
in the full afternoon sun. I could imagine the state she must
be in all too easily. How glad I was that I was out of the way!
Probably it was to help her in this degrading occupation that
she had called to me, and all for what purpose? To make the
idle Evans' life a little idler.

The afternoon was pleasant. I sat in the shade of a beech,

so still that a butterfly rested on a flower just by my hand, a little chalky-blue piece of finery. The sheep cropping the grass were clearly unaware that I was there. Across over the house and the dingle I could see the flag flying on Pentre Castle, which meant that Lord Pentre had come down from London. Beyond lay the Golfas, rising steeply, their sides clothed with oak, sycamore and fir, to those summits underneath which most of the midlands is laid out on one side like a map, while the other shows the jumbled, meaningless hills of Wales in wild and pointless confusion. It is to England that I look when I am dragged up there, as I have been, reluctantly, for you have to walk at least a part of the way up an unpleasantly steep path. There is, however, I must admit, something attractive in the Golfas, something which has compelled even me to consent to climb to the top of each point. Once, however, is quite enough.

I drank in the scene deeply. At moments of emotion one does notice one's surroundings vividly, clearly. Below me, my aunt was still wrestling, all unsuspectingly, with armfuls of pea-sticks. I glanced at my watch and observed with satisfaction that she was running her hospital meeting a bit fine. It would be all to the good if she had to hurry down the drive. Soon, however, she must go in and tidy up, preparatory to starting for that meeting to which, if my plans went right, she would never get. It was time for me to move.

Casually I got up and sauntered down the side of Yr Allt until I was out of sight of the house. Then I moved fast. Quickly I made my way below the bottom of the orchard. So well shall I always remember every detail of that afternoon that I recollect now, what I hardly observed then, that the apple trees gave every sign of a promising crop, but I could see no signs of damsons. I am glad of that. Damsons, to my mind, taste like boots stewed in ink. Pickled, however, they have a pleasant, sweet, but astringent flavor.

After coming out from the shelter of the orchard I had to be careful. This was the one point I had noticed in my earlier reconnaissance as being dangerous for a few yards. At the bottom of the orchard runs a little brook which goes pretty straight from there across the meadow in front of the lawn and joins the Brynmawr brook not far from the bridge. The slope of the lawn is continued across the meadow, and just before this little brook it drops quite steeply, so steeply as to be almost a bank, before rising again to a local crest, over which one can see four or five miles away the sides of the Broad Mountain. Directly I was behind this bank I should be out of sight once more, but on the way were a few open yards.

Seizing up So-so, partly for fear of stray cattle and partly to prevent his lingering across the dangerous gap, I shot quickly across from the corner of the orchard to the shelter of the bank of the little brook. So far as I could see all was well. Once behind the bank I made my way rapidly to the point I had settled on and placed the biscuit on the left of the road; So-so struggled in my arms, whined, and tried to lick my face as he saw his dainty as before put out for him. Fortunately, however, he did not bark. He knew that it would shortly be his. He could trust me. Then quick as lightning I crossed the road, fixed the string round So-so's collar and retired behind the tree hidden in the deep bracken. I had not realized before that crouching right down I should not be able actually to see the road. No matter, I could hear accurately enough. I was in time.

In fact I was a little early. I do not know how long, in fact, I had to wait. I suppose it was not really very long, but it seemed eternity to me, and I suppose to So-so too, waiting for the glad sound of "Paid for." The ironic correctness of those words suddenly appealed to my mind. "Paid for" indeed! How many insults were going to be paid for. I thought of the recent ones, of Williams and his fence, of Mary's blushing cheeks, of the frequent snubs, of Herbertson's sneers and Hughes' giggles; I thought further back of the frequent repressions of my childhod, of the everlasting "Don't, Edward" that pervaded all my nursery days. Ay, paid for, indeed. It was in a transcendental mood that I heard my aunt's car coming down the road, that I steeled my nerves to hold So-so back till I judged the exact second had arrived, and then with a loud shout or a hoarse whisper—I know not which—the words were said, the string was loosed.

From the road I heard, I could not see, a yell, a snap as the steering went, a howl from So-so, a grinding of brakes for a fraction of a second only, and then the sound of the car plunging off the road completely out of control.

I leapt to my feet to see the car disappearing over the edge of the bank. As it went I could see the door of the driver's seat being pushed open from inside and pushed back by the force of the air. Then the car disappeared from my sight.

Hurriedly I scrambled through the hedge. No one would object if I made a gap now; it is strange how such trivial thoughts will intrude at such moments. In front I could hear crashes and bangs as the car gained speed down the slope, cannoned sideways from tree trunk to tree trunk and, pitching over and over, eventually landed with a stunning thud at the bottom of the dingle. I was just in time to see the last crash. I do not think I shall ever forget it. It was tremendous in its unrestrained violence. The car seemed bent on dashing itself into the smallest possible fragments. There could not have been a bone unbroken in my aunt's body.

But my aunt had been partially successful in her attempt to get out of the car. In fact she had got out, but I could see that it had been of little avail. She had been thrown out violently and was lying limp and inert, with little more than her feet showing, her head buried in a tangled thicket of blackberries. I went down to her. Judging by her position and the stillness with which she lay, there could be little doubt. I am no doctor and I could not make any examination, but I was quite sure of the result. I cannot bear the thought of touching a dead body, so I left her alone. I am ashamed to say that I was a little sick.

It was not until I got back to the road that I realized that a tragedy had occurred. By the side of the road, his nose only an inch or two from his dearly loved biscuit, lay poor

So-so. It did not need any medical knowledge to see that he had gone. I must have let him loose a fraction of a second too late, the merest fraction, and heedless of the car he had dashed across the road and gained the other side, but that Juggernaut, plunging heedlessly on, had gone right over him. So-so would be my companion no more. I could not help recalling my aunt's phrase, that if he did not conform to her standards, she would "take action." She had indeed, even if involuntarily.

Poor So-so! Picking up the biscuit and casting it away into the nearest patch of brambles, I nerved myself to pick up his limp body and made my way back towards the house. It was no time to mourn his loss. It was a time for action. Worked up as I was, I could barely restrain my tears.

I had of course had the sense to think out exactly what I would do beforehand. I had deliberated whether it was best simply to remain absent and leave someone else to discover the accident, a course which would have the advantage of dissociating me entirely from it. But I had always felt that perhaps it would be wiser for me to be, if not an eyewitness, at any rate somewhere where I could have heard the crash. It was fortunate that I had based my plans on this idea, for So-so was seldom far from me, and since he, poor dear, had become so tragically involved with it, I must have been somewhere near.

Putting down his rapidly cooling form on a table wrapped in the duster my aunt kept in the hall, lest Athel and Thruthel should disturb his rest, I moved swiftly to the telephone.

"Llwll 47, quick—Dr. Spencer, please." I carefully made my voice sound agitated. "Dr. Spencer, come at once, please. An accident to her car, my aunt. Come quickly."

"In five minutes, Edward." Dr. Spencer wasted no time on words.

Turning round, to my annoyance, I found Cook at my elbow.

"Oh, Mr. Edward, what has happened? We thought we heard a crash."

It is at moments like these that it is so easy to make a mistake, so easy to appear to know something which it would really be impossible to know. I kept my head.

"I don't really know, Cook. So-so ran across the road in front of the gate and I heard a yell and a series of crashes. Miss Powell's car's at the bottom of the dingle; there is So-so." I pointed to the duster and saw Cook shudder.

"But, Miss Mildred?" she gasped.

"I don't know, Cook. I'm frightened. She must have been thrown out going down. She's—" I gave way to emotion.

"Oh, poor lady. You didn't never leave her? Oh, where is she, where is she? Let me get to her, let me go."

On the whole I thought it best that Dr. Spencer should find my aunt. "Calm yourself, Cook, Dr. Spencer's just coming."

"Then let's meet him on the road, it would save minutes for the precious lady. Run, Mr. Edward, run," and with that, Cook started to propel her fat body in an ungainly trot towards the front gate. Before, however, she had gone more than a few yards she stopped. "Better get Mary," she wheezed, "she's taken lessons with the Girl Guides in bandaging."

"All right, Cook. You get her. I'll go and fetch Evans. We might want someone to help carry her."

On the whole, let them all come was my feeling. They would distract attention from me; besides, if there were any signs left of my movements, they might be obliterated by the trampling of other people.

Returning with the gardener, I saw Cook and Mary in front of us opening the gate on to the road. Following them was the kitchen-maid, a grubby handkerchief applied to her eyes. Save for the girl's sobs we reached the bend of the drive in silence. I was rather sorry to see Spencer's car already drawn up on the side of the road. I should have liked to have had one more look round to see there was no possible clue lying about. However, I reassured myself quickly. It was extremely improbable. Indeed, what was there that could be incrim—careless.

The rest of the household got there before me, including Evans, who, from the moment I had called him, had moved incredibly fast for a man of his age. I found myself quite out of breath with the unusual exertion of running. From below came Spencer's voice.

"Come on, everybody, and help get Miss Powell out of this thicket. That's right, Mary, loosen that thorn from her dress. Come on, Edward. Don't stand doing nothing. Give a hand, man. This thorn bush may have saved her, but it's very hard to get her out of it. Youngish bush, fortunately, so that the boughs and the brambles have broken her fall, but were not too stiff. Good man, Evans, nearly free now. There we are." Thus talking volubly and encouraging everyone to exert himself, he supervised the operation of disentangling my aunt's form from the brambles and blackthorn bushes. For myself I thought it was obvious wisdom to exert myself to my utmost and, by the time the work was done, my clothes had been torn in several places and my face and hands were badly scratched. Eventually my aunt was extricated and laid out on as level a piece of ground as we could find. Dr. Spencer knelt down by her side instantly, and for a second there was complete silence. Then Cook began to sob quietly on Mary's shoulder and the kitchen-maid began to show every sign of having hysterics. I was curious to find that the reaction due to lack of employment after our exertion was affecting even me.

"Damn you, girl, keep quiet; and control yourself, Cook."

Spencer's voice was sharp and peremptory. He continued his examination, quickly but methodically. Suddenly he gave a grunt, then another as some further test was finished. I hoped he would not be long, for to tell the truth there would always be something incredibly ghastly about that particular spot in the dingle—not that I intended to stay at Brynmawr.

Spencer looked up. "She's alive, anyhow."

"Oh, my God!" The exclamation was torn from me. The whole world reeled round. Had I gone through all this for no purpose! I nearly fainted and had to sit down suddenly.

Spencer fortunately misunderstood my motives. "It's all right, Edward. Does you credit and all that, but I think I can give you a good report. Concussion, of course, and that sort of thing; but she's certainly alive and, as far as I can see, nothing broken. Too early to say yet; tell you that when we get her back to the house."

I looked down at my aunt's face, cruelly scratched by the blackberries. I remembered the crashing of the car and the pace it had attained before it reached the bottom of the dingle. I looked down and saw its remains. It seemed impossible that my aunt should have escaped, apparently comparatively lightly.

7

The rest of this evening has been torment.

I was, of course, very worked up at preparing my plan. There was bound to be a reaction from the nervous strain of the past few days. Had it succeeded there would have been a very difficult period to get over, until I had left Brynmawr for good. But as it has not, it is a thousand times worse. I am a prey to a thousand fears and anxieties lest some chance happening, some piece of inquisitiveness, some careless sentence should betray me. Of course I was prepared to face these in any case, but to face them for a while only, and with liberty to make my own plans for the future. But as it is, I cannot even do that. For it is abundantly clear that my whole scheme has been a failure. Not only is my aunt alive, she is not even seriously hurt.

I must be careful. That is why I am recording so fully every word and action, and why I propose to go on doing so. Let me continue then.

Eventually Evans and I got a door from an outhouse, and on that, precariously, her head supported by a collection of coats, we carried my aunt back. She was very heavy to get up the bank, and my coat is ruined by the blood from her cheek, but ultimately we managed to get her up. That brute

Spencer would not allow us a second's rest on the way. That
is another point to be remembered if I ever get a chance to
settle accounts with him.

While he carried on his ministrations upstairs, I went down
to my own room and sat there gasping. Presently in came
Cook, forgetful, apparently, in the crisis, of her normal routine and position in the house.

"I've brought you a nice cup of hot tea, Mr. Edward, very
strong." Indeed she had, only unfortunately most of it was
in the saucer. "There's nothing like a nice cup of tea when
you feel funny. Mary and I have both had one and we feel
heaps better. You try it," she added, noticing my reluctance.
I always take my tea very weak. If possible, I take China with
a slice of lemon, and this curious dark-brown liquid did not
look appetizing.

"You try it," repeated Cook. "Mary was all for bringing in
the drawing-room tea, but of course I know you couldn't
touch food now."

Just in time I realized that I ought to be a little abnormal.
It had been on the tip of my tongue to say that I saw no
reason for not having my ordinary tea, but I quickly decided
that this would be a mistake. Cook would think it unfeeling
of me. I saw I must sacrifice myself once more. I swallowed
the sickly liquid and, to my surprise, found that it did have
a steadying effect on my nerves.

Cook, quite disregarding the social *convenances*, continued
to chatter on. She was evidently anxious—a curious but in-
variable trait in her class—to gossip about the whole thing.
This would never do. The fewer people I talked to about it
the safer.

"I'm sorry, Cook." I managed a weak smile. "But I can't
bear to talk about it."

"Poor lamb!" (The patronizing airs of the woman!) "I can
well understand. And you seeing it too."

That I mustn't pass. "Not quite, Cook. But do you mind?"
I handed her back the cup and, sitting in an arm-chair, I
put my head in my hands. Cook departed. I don't think she

could well do anything else. I lit a cigarette and considered the problem. The more I thought of it the more reassured I was. So far as I could see there was no reason whatever why even suspicion should turn towards me whatever had happened. At that time, of course, I did not know how lightly my aunt had got off.

After some long interval, I heard Spencer come down the stairs and then go up again, I suppose to give some instructions to Mary, and then come down once more. I quickly removed my diary to its appointed drawer. By the time he came in, I was getting out of a chair to meet him and ask his news.

"All very good, Edward. Marvelously and unbelievably good. She's regained consciousness, she's not damaged in the least, and after a few days' rest and quiet she'll be her normal self again. Just as she was before."

I sat down. There was the devil of it. My aunt was to be "just as she was before," and this idiotic old man told me that as if he was bringing me wonderfully good news, and I mustn't even show how foolish I thought him. Just as before, indeed. No, So-so would lie between us and prevent things from ever being just as before. But Spencer was speaking again.

"I wish you'd tell me just what happened." He sat down opposite to me and began to fill his pipe. "Your telephone message is all the information I've got so far."

This must be faced. Cook could be brushed aside, but some time or other I must give an account to someone. It would look curious to try and avoid all conversation about it now that I knew of and had to feign relief at the lightness of my aunt's injuries.

"I hardly know." I spoke slowly, as if trying to reconstruct what I had seen accurately. At the same time I was going to have seen very little! "I was walking across the meadow in front of the house with my dog—"

"Your dog?" and Dr. Spencer apparently did not associate dogs with me. "Oh, your Pekingese?"

Well, what does he call a Pekingese? A cat? I restrained myself. "You, As I say, we were going across the meadow in the front of the house—"

"What were you doing there?"

"Oh, just walking across it, when—"

"But why walk across it? Where from?"

This was tiresome but Spencer always asks foolish questions. He's about as bad in his general conversation as when he plays bridge. I could see that it would be wiser to go back to the beginning.

"I was sitting this afternoon on Yr Allt, admiring the view and reading. Shortly before four o'clock I thought I would like to see how the apples were doing in the orchard. Some of them hang right over the hedge into the field beyond, so I strolled down the side of Yr Allt and looked at them, and even went into the field. That put into my head the idea that the best way back would be across the meadow and the lawn instead of through the orchard." Here I was on thin ice, for through the orchard is shorter and avoids getting over a fence. Besides, I had to think of a reason for going to the other end of the meadow by the road. But I had had ready in advance a brilliant idea for this.

"On the way across I thought I saw some mushrooms—"

"My dear Edward, I've lived in these parts many years longer than you and there's never been a mushroom on that meadow to my certain knowledge during my lifetime, certainly not as early as this."

"Hasn't there, Dr. Spencer?" My surprise was well done, considering I knew he was right, but had not thought he knew so much. "Anyhow, I thought I saw some. When I got near the fence two things happened, apart from the fact that there were no mushrooms—"

"What did you mistake for them?"

"Stones, or perhaps white flowers, or just a trick of light. I don't know. Perhaps there was a stray piece of paper. Anyhow, as I neared the fence, firstly poor So-so must have—"

"I can't imagine any of those things being there."

"Poor So-so must have thought," I went on firmly, "that he saw a rabbit going through the fence. At the same moment I heard a car going along the road. So-so disappeared, and I heard a yell from my aunt and a howl from poor So-so. I ran to the fence just in time to see the car going over the edge. It went out of my sight, but I heard it cannoning down the bank from tree to tree. As I reached the top I saw it crash into the bottom of the dingle with a sickening thud. At first I thought my aunt must still be in it, then I thought I saw her where she was, in fact; then I noticed So-so lying dead"—there was a catch in my voice which I could not avoid—"by the side of the road, and then I thought I'd better telephone you and get the household to come and help. That's really all I know."

Spencer considered silently for a minute. "I'm sorry about your Pekingese," he said ultimately and a little awkwardly. "You were very fond of him, weren't you?" I nodded. Fond, indeed! I adored So-so. "Why didn't you go down and extricate your aunt at once?"

"What good could I have done, Dr. Spencer? I'm not a doctor, and getting her out of those bushes was a job for more than one person."

"So it proved, but I should have thought your instinct would have been to have gone down at once to see if you could do anything. However, perhaps the best thing was to get hold of me at once."

"I didn't waste a minute. I thought that was right."

"Lucky thing you found me in." He smiled meditatively. Apparently he thought he had done something clever merely by being in.

"Yes, and you must have driven fast, Doctor. I didn't know your old bus would go so well." We were emerging on to safer topics.

"Yes, an average of thirty-five to forty miles an hour is nothing in many places, but it's terrific in this country-side. Five past four you got me and it wasn't ten past when I got out of the car." A sudden thought seemed to strike him.

"Wasn't she going to the hospital meeting?" I nodded. "Well, she'd have been late for it for the first time for over ten years."

"She was pulling up some pea-sticks in the garden. I saw her doing it from the hill and I expect that made her run it a bit fine. Perhaps, too, that made her hurry."

"Perhaps. Well, anyhow, I'll leave you now. Cook and Mary are going to help with looking after her tonight and I'm going to collect the District Nurse and bring her round. She's putting her things together now, but we shan't, I expect, need her for long. I'll be in tomorrow, Edward. Good night. Hullo, what's this? Oh, your Pekingese! Poor little brute. You know, Edward, he was really the villain of the piece; oh, I don't mean it hardly. He intended no harm, but all the same he jolly nearly killed your aunt. I shouldn't leave him here. 'Bury him deep, he won't keep. Bury him well, or he'll smell.' Good night."

Heartless brute. I saw him out of the front door. In a minute he was back.

"Got any apples, by the way?"

"Yes, quite a lot. But no damsons."

"Good night."

"Good night."

This time he really was gone. Lucky thing that I had actually noticed those damson trees. There is no end to the questions that inquisitive old fool can ask!

3: *"Somnoquubes"*

LIFE is slipping back superficially into its normal routine. My aunt's convalescence was incredibly rapid—her vitality is really amazing. Her car will shortly be replaced. But So-so cannot be replaced. And so, though things may appear to be the same, they never will be. One more wrong has to be righted. So-so has to be avenged. I am more determined than ever. Chance and a blackthorn bush have ruined my first plan. I shall think of a second.

In one way, though, I think I may take credit—there has been no inquiry, no unpleasant suspicions. My plan was perfectly sound in that respect. There is therefore no reason why, provided I work it out with equal care, a second plan should not be equally watertight so far as I am concerned, more successful in its results. I shall think of one soon.

My aunt's own reaction to the accident was typical. She listened quite silently, lying in an arm-chair in that hideous drawing-room, an emerald-green scarf round her shoulders clashing violently with the carpet, and until I had finished she made no comment.

"And you mean to say, Edward, that you left me hanging like an overripe blackberry, while you went back to the house and telephoned to Dr. Spencer, simply because you didn't like the idea of touching a corpse. Oh, don't shudder at plain speaking. You thought I was dead and so off you go. You're able to carry back the body of your toy dog and wrap it up carefully in a duster, but you can't touch your aunt. Oh, yes, I heard how carefully So-so was looked after. It's rather a contrast, my dear. Then I suppose you lit a cigarette, had a drink and finally decided you'd better ring up the doctor. Charming of you. I wonder you didn't solve a crossword puzzle first. Oh, but you don't do crosswords, do you? Well, you *might* have written a sonnet on the event then, while you could still capture your first emotions."

"Really, Aunt Mildred, you're most unfair. I still think I was right to ring up Dr. Spencer at once, before trying to get you out of the bush. And I may say he agrees with me."

"Does he? I wonder! It rather depends on whether you saw me fall softly or heavily."

"I wasn't sure about that."

"No, I notice you seem a bit muddled. You gave the doctor the impression that you saw the car go over the top and then didn't see it again till you saw it reach the bottom, and that's the idea I should have got too from what you have just said, but at the time you said to Cook that you saw me thrown out."

"No, Aunt Mildred, I told Cook that I thought you had been thrown out, because I thought I saw you lying in the bush, but I didn't actually see you fall. I remember Cook had got it wrong later and I had to correct her."

My aunt looked at me keenly. "I see, dear. That just clears up a little muddle. But I still think it was intolerable of you to leave me like that without looking to see if you could do anything at once."

"I'm sorry you feel that way about it, Aunt. Supposing I'd lifted you up the wrong way? I might have damaged something. Really, I think still, and of course thought then, that I acted for the best."

"Well, if I can't get you to see it my way, we must leave it where it is. It does stick in my mind that you were a little callous. However, we'll leave it like that and say no more about it."

I know of nothing more irritating than being told that "we'll say no more about it." It always implies that the speaker is in the right, obviously and demonstrably, to anyone except the obstinate listener, that the speaker is full of Christian charity of which he or she is using a large supply by refraining from turning the other person's defeat into a rout, and finally that the speaker has, in fact, said everything he wants to say, and is merely anxious to prevent the other person producing his arguments.

Conversation ceased between us for some time and I resumed the novel I had been reading. The rain was dripping down steadily outside and the room was cheerless and damp. I should have liked a fire, but fires at Brynmawr are regulated strictly by the calendar and not by the temperature. My own room would have been warmer and more aesthetically pleasing, but there was a sort of theory that my aunt had a claim on the attentions of everyone until she was completely well, which, in fact, she already was. Accordingly I sat in her uncomfortable and ugly chair and listened to the loud tick of the very shabby clock and the drip of the rain as it ran down a pipe into a water-bucket.

Presently the silence was broken by my aunt.

"There's one other matter, Edward, I'm afraid I must speak to you about, though I'm afraid you won't like it."

I have never known anything so broached that there was the least possibility of my liking. However. "And that is?"

"I rather welcome seeing a little sentiment in you, Edward. In some ways you are a little hard; but you mustn't make a fool of yourself about So-so. Now, don't jump up like that and fly into a pet, just listen reasonably. No dog in this house ever has a tombstone. It was bad enough your making Evans dig up the garden for him; still worse when you made a sort of coffin and even conducted some kind of a burial service over him, from what I hear. That was bad enough, but I refuse absolutely to have a tombstone in the potatoes, and I absolutely and entirely refuse to have an epitaph beginning" —my aunt produced a piece of paper from her handbag and adjusted her spectacles—" 'To darling So-so, his master's only joy. A victim of speed,' and going on, 'Who dreads to the dust

returning? Who shrinks from the sable shore, where the high
and haughty yearning, of the soul can sting no more?' Really,
Edward."

I blushed at the way my aunt read out the four lines in a
sing-song voice, accentuating the rhythm, but depriving the
words of all sense. One does not like what is sacred to oneself to be mocked at by others.

"And why not? So-so's whole life *was* a high and haughty
yearning. I spent a long time finding something suitable."

"My dear Edward, it's merely ridiculous. Besides, he was
not a 'victim of speed.' He never ran really fast in his life if
that is what you mean, and if you imply that he was the
victim of my driving, in the first place it isn't true, and in the
second place, if it were, I won't have it thrust into my notice
amongst my own vegetables. And that, Edward, is that."

"Very well, then. I shall find somewhere else, if there is
any square inch of this country-side which I can call my
own, and there I shall bury him and myself erect his tombstone."

"I shouldn't. If you put it up, it'll be sure to fall down. But
leaving that aside, you won't do anything of the kind because
Morgan won't cut it for you."

So it was that wretched stone-mason who had told my aunt!
"He told me he would, but I should not be surprised if he
broke his word. All these people round here do."

My aunt slapped a cushion violently. "When will you remember, Edward, that you're a Welshman, and that by these
constant sneers at them you only run yourself down?"

I turned a contemptuous glance on my aunt. "Some of us
manage to outgrow the disadvantages with which we start."

My aunt considered this for a moment. "And some of us
never grow out of the nursery stage."

I did not deign to answer this, but I know quite well that if
my aunt has got at Morgan, I shall not get my tombstone cut.
Perhaps I can get it done elsewhere later. I shall see about it
next time I get out of this prison. Or perhaps I can wait until
after my second attempt, and then have him reburied near

where he died; or would it be tactless to call attention to it any more? Perhaps.

2

We had what my aunt regards as quite an important festivity tonight. That is to say the Spencers—all of them—came to dinner. Anything duller I find hard to imagine, but my aunt is convinced that she is providing life, amusement, and gaiety for me—which is hard to bear.

I think that Mrs. Spencer is one of the strangest guests it is possible to have. In her own home she is just passively feeble, terribly anxious that you should be properly entertained, and always suffering from an inferiority complex that you will go away and criticize her arrangements. There is generally, in consequence, a great deal lacking; for one thing, one always feels that one is being a nuisance to the woman, and for another thing, one is always bored. At least I am, but to my aunt all things Spencerian are perfect. As a result, I have mainly kept my opinions to myself, and so have to suffer the overbearing doctor, his futile wife, and hearty son *ad nauseam.* Freed from her own domestic worries though, one would have thought that Mrs. Spencer would have been able to look the world in the face and cheer up a little. Not a bit of it however. She always seems to be completely absent-minded and takes no interest whatever in what is going on, except to give occasional glances of worship at her husband or her son, whom she regards as the two most wonderful beings in existence. For a long while I could not make out what she was thinking about whenever she was away from her own house, until I realized that she was one of those people who are constantly haunted by a fear that she has left the bathroom tap running or shut the cat up in the larder. This evening, clad in pale lavender, a dress I have seen I tremble to think how many times, she was peculiarly distrait. She seemed hardly able to look me in the face, and

started visibly whenever I addressed a remark to her. She
must have been fearing some appalling calamity in the do
mestic circle. It really would have been a kindness to have
let her talk about it. She seemed to have recollected the
trouble almost immediately she left her own house, for when
I came down a few minutes after they had arrived, and said
good evening to her, she jumped violently as if she had the
most appallingly guilty conscience. And though the woman is
dull, I'm sure she never had done anything to be ashamed
of in her life; she hasn't enough go in her.

Apparently my entry had caused a break in some conversation the other four were having—probably discussing
me; it's a way my aunt has—but I soon managed to start some
other subject. I flatter myself on my *savoir-faire*. As a matter
of fact there was a subject I wanted to start, or rather on
which I wanted to pick young Spencer's brains, and I had
decided to do it in public! *Toujours l'audace!* Done openly,
no one would ever suspect my motives. Sure enough the talk
during dinner veered around to a case which was exciting a
good deal of interest at the time, in which a group of people
were accused of setting fire deliberately to obsolete stock in
order to defraud Insurance Companies.

"From what I know of them," said young Spencer, "most
Insurance Companies jolly well deserve to be robbed. They're
a shocking lot of robbers themselves, and never pay up if
they can possibly help it."

"Don't be cynical, Jack. My Insurance Company have paid
over my car like lambs."

"And why not, Aunt dear?" I wanted to turn the conversation to a different by-path, and this, I thought, was a good
moment. The Doctor was looking very hard at his plate, and
Mrs. Spencer was suffering from some peculiarly dreadful
paroxysm of doubt. I continued: "But what always beats me
is how they start these fires. It seems so clever of them, but I
suppose it's simple if you know how."

"Quite, I suppose." The Doctor's tone rather damped con-
tinuance of the subject, but I was not to be denied.

"All the same, I suppose none of us here knows how to do it—unless you do, Jack."

"I—why should I?"

"Well, don't they teach you in your Territorials how to blow up dumps, or put down delayed action mines or something like that? After all, I suppose the principle's the same."

Jack Spencer's cypher face of rounded foolishness—the best phrase Tennyson ever used—expressed blank astonishment. "But, my dear fellow, I'm in the Infantry, not the Engineers."

How like the Territorials! They're never useful. I had been counting on young Spencer to give me the information I wanted. At this moment, however, I received an unexpected ally in old Spencer.

"All the same, Jack, it would be very useful to know how to destroy any works or material you had to leave behind in a retreat, and you can't always count on having the R.E. to help you. Don't they tell you somewhere something about it? Manual of Field Engineering, for instance? The Boche used that trick an awful lot when they fell back to the Hindenburg line in '17. Nasty business it was too."

I chipped in quickly lest the rest of dinner should become a chapter from old Spencer's unpublished war reminiscences, a subject of incredible dullness.

"But I suppose your textbooks, like all other textbooks, never teach you anything useful?"

"Don't be stupid, Edward. I'm sure they're excellent books."

Now what could my aunt know about it? Jack Spencer looked in a startled way from his father to her, and succeeded in splashing some gravy onto his shirt front. This however, I felt, was not of great importance. That shirt should have gone to the laundry in my opinion before that evening, not after. However, it would have to go now.

"I suppose I could find out somehow," he said. "I don't think it's very difficult. I think this fellow we were talking about did it with a clock."

82   *The Murder of My Aunt*

"A clock?" said I. "How?" For a moment I had a curious impression that Mrs. Spencer was about to try to stop the conversation, but changed her mind after a glance at her husband. Young Jack continued:

"Oh, you put a little bit of solder somewhere on the face of the clock so that when the hands get to a certain hour the connection's made."

He seemed inclined to stop, but once more old Spencer prompted him. Really the old man was being quite useful! I could almost feel inclined to like him for once!

"Connection to what?" went on Jack, answering his father's question. "Oh, to a battery, or to the electric-light system, if you choose, I believe. You can just fit the two wires of your circuit into a plug in the wall."

"But what starts the fire?" I asked.

Jack made a futile attempt to remove the gravy-stain which he had only just noticed. He became a little vague.

"Oh, you don't make your circuit entirely of wire that carries the current properly. You break it with a bit of thin wire which will glow—I'm not sure what kind of wire, but anyhow, something that gets red hot."

"But a glow isn't a fire, Jack."

"No, Miss Powell, but you put something on top of the thin wire which will catch fire if it's touched by anything hot."

"What, just a bit of paper?" I put in. This sounded too easy!

"No. I don't think that's good enough. This fellow used some kind of celluloid substance, but I'm not quite sure what. The Engineers, I believe, use shredded gun-cotton."

"Bravo, Jack. You do seem to know a good deal about it. Apparently your textbooks are better than Edward thinks."

My short-lived admiration for the doctor died away quickly, but apparently the conversation was too much for Mrs. Spencer.

"I think it's a horrid thing to talk about," she broke in. "We might all be burnt in our beds the way you're all talking.

These horrible infernal machines. You're going to the County Show, of course, Mildred dear?"

But Mrs. Spencer's well-meant attempt to turn the conversation was not entirely successful. Her husband headed her off from the County Show to another topic.

"By the way, talking of machines, Miss Powell, I was looking at the clock on the remains of your old car today. Herbertson showed it to me. It had stopped at seven minutes to four, so you wouldn't have been late for that hospital meeting, after all." He turned to me. "Must preserve your aunt's reputation for punctuality, you know, Edward. You may have noticed that she's rather particular about it. Especially at breakfast time, eh, Edward?" He changed a sly tone for a boisterous laugh.

I should have wanted to have put a pin in the bubble of that reputation anyhow, but remembering him saying that he noticed that I had rung him up on that afternoon at five past four, it was necessary to do something about it. The news was rather staggering, but I kept my head, and quick as thought went straight for the difficulty. *Toujours l'audace, toujours l'audace!*

"I don't think that can be right, or I should have got through to you on the phone sooner than I did. Sorry to spoil your reputation, Aunt, but I remember noticing the day before that that clock was a good five minutes slow."

My aunt looked at me angrily, almost disdainfully. "Really, Edward, I have no such recollection."

If we had not had visitors I could see we should have had a row, merely because she was not prepared to admit that she might possibly have been late for her wretched meeting. What conceit that woman has!

The conversation returned to the County Show, and ultimately, many weary hours afterwards, those boring Spencers departed. But it had been for me a very successful evening. Firstly, I had dealt naturally and in my stride with the tiresome and unexpected little point of the clock on the old

Morris. Secondly, I had learnt that the Insurance Company had not made any difficulties as to my aunt's claim, and that meant that neither Herbertson, their agent, nor they, had noticed anything curious in the steering gear or the brake cables. It would indeed have been odd if they had, seeing how completely smashed up the car was. Still, it was a relief. And thirdly, I had got a great deal of very good information quite casually from young Spencer's description of the use of clocks for starting fires. Acting on his hints I could work out the rest. Perhaps it was a pity that Mrs. Spencer had actually mentioned "burning in their beds," but with luck the unfortunate remark would be forgotten. I wonder what put the idea into her head? It has been in mine for some time now, an offshoot partly of this fire trial, and partly of my previous idea of an explosion in the petrol tank, which I see now would have been a better idea. Fire! Fire! Beautiful tongues of living, leaping, dancing flame, destroying everything, obliterating everything. I see now that my earlier dreams were right. Those flames dwell with me night and day.

3

It is a pity that one is never taught anything useful at school. Not that I remained very long at any school, or ever took more than a casual interest, unless I was obliged to, in any of the dreary subjects put down in the curriculum. I could see very early on that it was impossible to work sympathetically with teachers whose minds were so narrow, and whose whole spirit was so tiresome and fatiguing.

But one never knows what may be useful to one. It has already been awkward that I have had to discuss the question of setting fire to things with the Spencers, and though I flatter myself that I did it so casually that the conversation will not be remembered, yet I would have liked to have known it all for myself. And anyhow, my information is by no means complete, and I shall have to carry out experiments, always a difficult thing to do with so inquisitive a person as my aunt about. Moreover I want to know something about sleeping draughts.

Today, therefore, in the pursuit of knowledge—it's wonderful how this sort of thing sharpens up one's intelligence—I went shopping. Local gossip being so terrific, I took the precaution, not only of avoiding Llwll, naturally, but even of omitting Abercwm. Shrewsbury, however, I felt was large enough to forget my trivial purchases. They consisted of a cheap clock, a boy's set for soldering things (it was touching how solicitous an uncle I was in this purchase!), some lengths of electric flex, some very thin wire, alleged to be for the hanging of miniatures on a wall in which I did not wish to drive nails, and where I wanted the wire to be almost invisible, a small electric battery (for experiments only; when it comes to the point I shall use the electric-light system, for which the Brynmawr brook provides an inadequate supply of power), a hundred shot-gun cartridges, several very ugly celluloid toys (dear uncle again for a younger and equally imaginary nephew), and a copy of a medical paper with a repellent name suggesting the painful operations which befall those who come into the clutches of Spencer's fraternity. This business is getting expensive..

All these I shall keep locked up in the tool-box of La Joyeuse. I simply dare not conduct any experiments in the house except one dress rehearsal, so to speak. But there are plenty of by-roads and lanes near by to which I can drive and pursue my researches without the least chance of being molested or observed.

As I drove back to Brynmawr, a little incident occurred which proved to me how necessary it was that I should keep well away from prying eyes. I found Williams staring intently at the spot where my aunt had met with her accident. I was compelled to slow down because his dog would not get out of the way, and so I could not avoid a conversation with him; besides, I was rather anxious to know what he was doing there.

"Good morning to you, Mr. Edward," came his singsong voice. "It was indeed a grand mercy to all of us that Miss Powell was not injured. Look you, she has asked me to see what can be done that no one shall go over here again. She says it is not enough that we have white posts to mark it at night, but there must be something which will prevent it. She will not have iron fencing here, or hurdles, look you, because, indeed, she says she will not have the view spoilt."

"Why not plant a hedge then?"

"Indeed, yes, but it will not grow in three weeks, and Miss Powell seems nervous after her—" he paused as if at loss for a word "—adventure. Perhaps it will be best if I bank up the road, I think, and yes, perhaps it can be done. But indeed, Mr. Edward, you should not have thrown that biscuit to your dog, for it is looking for another he must have been that made him cross the road so. And poor dog, he was killed, and Miss Powell, she was indeed nearly killed too— and for a biscuit whatever." His change of subject in the middle had been a bit startling, but I showed no surprise.

"Oh, nonsense, Williams. I believe I did once chuck poor So-so a biscuit somewhere near here, but he wouldn't expect to find another there just because he'd once had one here. I think he was chasing a rabbit."

"It may be so, but it was just here that I talked to your small brown dog before while he ate a biscuit."

"Did you? Oh, well, the world's full of coincidences." I looked at my watch. "Well, I mustn't keep my aunt waiting for her lunch," and I glided on, having, I hope, kept my tone as light as the movement of La Joyeuse.

But I hope that old fool will keep his mouth shut!

This afternoon I have been reading this medical paper; at least, the advertisements, and very odd reading they are. I have, for a long while past, realized that several little pains of mine have been entirely neglected by old Spencer, and now, fortunately, I can obtain the remedies. I must buy this thing more often. But I have had to change my mind as to one opinion I have long held. I was once told that the wording of advertisements was written by people called "advertising agents," a vulgar lot of people. These things are obviously too learned for them to have composed. I wonder who does do it? I mean sentences beginning: "In sepsis followed by extreme leucopenia or neutropenia—" or "composed of Staphylococcus aureus and Bacillus acnes—" must be written by very clever men.

But best of all I did find in it what I was seeking for. What I really wanted to know was whether a mere layman could walk into a chemist's and buy a sleeping draught. Naturally I did not find a direct answer to that. I did not expect to. Of course the simplest way to find out was to go to the nearest chemist and try to buy one. One would find out and possibly get the stuff, but I was afraid to do this in case the chemist should start making inquiries. It might be part of the law that he should. Anyhow, I was not going to risk it within a hundred miles of Brynmawr. In London, perhaps, one could give a wrong address.

But I felt that if, instead of asking vaguely for something to put one to sleep, I was able to ask for a definite product, it would sound so much more convincing. It would be easy to get hold of a sheet of Dr. Spencer's note-paper and write a letter recommending its use for myself under some other name. Probably no such formality was necessary, and I hoped it would not be necessary to produce the letter, but it would be wise to be prepared. I know so little about these things. As I said before, school education is appallingly deficient.

Anyhow, in this matter the paper did not let me down, for here, fortunately, was something, the very newest and latest idea—little tablets which could be put into any liquid and would dissolve at once and be taken without the patient knowing. Apparently the great thought was to avoid offending the susceptibilities of the patient, a very proper, worthy, and meritorious wish. And these Somnoquubes were guaranteed to ensure really sound sleep. Apart from the fact that I dislike seeing "cubes" spelt "quubes," I was all in favor of it.

Things are working out nicely.

4

The great disadvantage of the plan I have in mind is that practically everything I possess will be destroyed. I have got a small insurance on my personal belongings. I took it out because I found that sparks fly out so easily from the wood fires we have, and once or twice dozing in front of the fire on a winter's afternoon a small hole has been burnt in the leg of my trousers before I detected the presence of the spark, and of course that ruins the suit, for I cannot wear patched clothes, even in the depths of this desert.

But the policy is only for a small amount, and it will not start to cover all the clothes I have, a wardrobe, I may say, chosen with great care and taste. I suppose it is replaceable, and certainly nothing is more interesting than buying clothes —one can spend hours planning it—but all the same I hate the idea of losing things which I have taken such trouble to collect and to match. Besides, there is always the financial question. Degrading, but true.

And besides clothes, I have other things. There are my books, for instance. Many of the most charming I have bought in France and brought through the customs with difficulty. I might not be able to get them again, for these things, little masterpieces though they are in their own way, are gossamer trifles that appeal not to the many-headed and, naturally neglected by the multitude, drift away down the breeze of time. I have never met a best-seller yet that I have managed to finish. It is not surprising. One's taste is, I hope, superior to the average.

I have been looking through them carefully. I might take away nominally two or three with me—for of course I shall be away when the fire occurs—and actually I suppose I could manage a dozen without making my shelves unduly bare, supposing my aunt were to notice their bareness; and the trouble is that she might so well notice that sort of thing, for, apart from the natural inquisitiveness I have commented on before, she has brought the art of poking her nose in where she is not wanted to a high pitch of perfection. Besides, I have a strong suspicion that she reads them in secret, for I am sure that she is really as much of a hypocrite as all these people who are given to good works and the Galahad pose, and directly I am away she might start in to contemplate her favorite piece of debauchery and find it missing. I must admit that one or two of them are extremely realistic. If my aunt does read them, it is perhaps just as well that her knowledge of French will prevent her from appreciating the more subtle nuances of the more interesting *double ententes*.

But be that as it may, it is highly undesirable that her suspicions should be awakened for, unlike the arrangement with her car, it would be very awkward if a search were made in my bedroom and my preparations discovered. Especially as I shall have to use the battery. I tried an experiment with the electric light just once the other night and unfortunately it blew all the fuses in the house. I can't think what I did wrong, but it was very alarming. Fortunately it was in the middle of the night, so I had plenty of time to put everything away, since no one knew at the time, of course, that anything had happened. I was terrified, though, that I might have started a fire before I intended to! However, after rather an anxious time, I came to the conclusion that all was well, but it was very late before I went to sleep.

Then the next day there was a difficulty. Evans is the only one of the Brynmawr household who is allowed to repair the lighting, and if the discovery that the fuse had gone was left until the ordinary time for turning on the lights, he would have gone home. His cottage is about half a mile away, but that half-mile involves going down the dingle behind the house and up most of the other side. Evans, of course, could come back easily, but I had an uneasy feeling that I should be the person sent to fetch him, in the dark too. Accordingly, I thought I had better make the discovery myself earlier in the day, I thought I might as well kill two birds with one stone, so seeing my aunt doing up a parcel in the hall, I adopted my most winning manner.

"Surely you can't see to do that up, can you, Aunt? Let me turn on the light. You mustn't strain your eyes, you know. It's so easy to do when one's not so young."

And of course the light didn't go on. Simple. I had to stand a snubbing from my aunt who seemed to resent the implication that she was not still in her teens, but my point was achieved. It was so easy to carry on. "Hullo, what's wrong with the light?" and to stroll in a nonchalant manner into the dining-room and find that the switch wouldn't work there either, and then with a gradual crescendo of surprise discover that none of the lights would work, and so send Mary for Evans.

All the while my aunt continued to do up her parcels. "Why can't you go yourself?" was her only comment. As she had the end of the string in her mouth I made her repeat it before I would admit I heard, and that sort of remark never sounds so biting when you say it a second time.

The parcels, however, suggested rather a bright idea. I took the bull by the horns and, sitting on the oak chest in the hall, swinging the neatly pointed toe of a brown shoe, I dropped a few casual remarks to my aunt which, had she but known, were pregnant with her fate.

"I'm spending a few days with Innes next week, Aunt Mildred."

"Innes? Oh, yes, that rather unpleasant friend of yours with a Bentley he can't drive. Well, as long as he doesn't come here, I don't mind. We should probably have to repaint the whole house next time—unless he knocked it down completely."

"How absurd you are! A little mathematical demonstration would prove to you that the room you have left, or rather built up at enormous cost" (that's what sticks in my aunt's throat, the excessive cost of that useless way past the house, entirely due to her desire to use local labor—indeed I believe the whole thing was my aunt's local relief works for Llwll—as if she was the government!) "is far too narrow for Guy's car."

"Guy? Oh, Mr. Innes. Well, anyhow, he scraped the paint off the house. There isn't any paint on that chest, Edward, and it *is* oak; all the same, if you go on kicking it you'll take the polish off it and perhaps do more harm than that. If you can't stand for a moment, sit on a chair for heaven's sake, or perhaps you won't do any damage on the stairs if you keep the whole of you on the carpet." And here she began to make a coarse comparison between the breadth of the carpet and the room I occupy when I sit down, which I will not repeat.

"Well, anyhow, I shall go next Tuesday. I thought it would be a good opportunity to take some suits I want pressed and cleaned into Shrewsbury. Drop them on the way and pick them up on the way back. And then the binding of some of my books needs attention, so I'll take them in at the same time."

My aunt stared at me. "And since when have you decided to go to the expense of having your clothes pressed outside?"

"Since I came to the conclusion, if you must know, Aunt Mildred, that neither you nor Mary press them very well. Besides, you can't *clean* them—now, can you?"

"No, that's true, *but* that's quite settled all question of pressing them at home for ever until you take that remark back and apologize, Edward."

" 'The elementary laws never apologize, neither do I apologize,' " I quoted flippantly.

"No apology, baggy knees then. And you know, Edward, a fat person always bulges his clothes more than a thin one. However, just as you please. Your gratitude for the trouble we have spent in ironing your wretched suits is touching, but as for those dirty books of yours—I should have thought a little filth outside would have matched the inside. Still, please yourself. You seem to be getting very rich all of a sudden." My aunt slapped down on the table the last parcel. "Ah, Evans, here you are. Master Edward's fused all the lights."

"My dear Aunt, I only tried out of the kindness of my heart, which does not seem to be appreciated, to turn on the light to save your eyes and found it wouldn't go on. Then, having a little common sense, I tried the others and found they wouldn't, either. Why that should be called 'fusing the lights' I can't think. You don't even know" (I picked my pronouns rather neatly) "that the lights are fused at all. It may be something else. And why say I fused them? It's typical, but hardly fair."

My aunt did have the grace to blush, so far as she can.

"Sorry, Edward, I'm afraid I was rather jumping to conclusions."

She really seemed quite confused. No doubt it was very unpleasant for her to have to apologize. Indeed an apology was a joy I seldom extracted from her, and one that was all the sweeter because, had the old fool known, I *had* fused them. However, I would show her I could be dignified.

"That's quite all right. Let's forget about it, and meanwhile, perhaps Evans will put the lights right."

Quite a successful morning. It will be extraordinary how many books need rebinding, and how many suits need cleaning! All the same, I wish I had stuck to the point about cleaning and not mentioned the way my clothes are pressed for me here, because, in fact, Mary or my aunt do them quite adequately, and it does save quite a lot of trouble and expense. But there I go again. I keep on forgetting that I am not going to live here much longer, and so it doesn't matter.

5

After all, I ran quietly into Shrewsbury on the Monday evening. La Joyeuse does not—bless her—hold a great quantity of luggage, and had I taken all the luggage that I intended to take in addition to the suits and books, I should have been hard put to it to find room for it all. Besides, the overloading of the car would have been rather obvious and I did not, as I said before, want to cause any comment.

I have had, as it is, to do one thing which is a trifle unusual, but very likely it will escape comment. I have locked the wardrobe and taken the key away. I thought of using a drawer in my dressing-table, but I couldn't get the pile built up nicely in it. Besides, Mary would have been certain to have noticed it when she tidied up my room, whereas I have taken good care that there shall be no reason for her going to the wardrobe. I never do lock the drawers of the dressing-table. I have, you see, a little stoutly built safe which my aunt provided for me many years ago when I first began to possess things which were better locked up, but which I did not wish to keep in the bank. It has been very useful as the hiding place for these precious pages. (Of course I have taken them with me and am writing this at Guy's.) Ah, how I wonder what is happening now at Brynmawr! If I was not so many miles away I think I should be climbing up to the roof and straining my eyes for the sight of that bright blaze which I so confidently hope is now raging.

I can imagine the scene this evening. Everything will have gone on quite naturally until after dinner. I suppose my aunt does have dinner when I am away? So many women left to themselves have dreadful scratch meals—on the whole, I expect she does. She has a very proper respect for the conventions, and incidentally a perfectly good appetite. Besides, one of the old curses should this time stand me in good stead. There always has been dinner at Brynmawr on Tuesday evenings, so there always will be. Therefore my aunt will have dinner in solemn state, and after dinner, coffee. That's when things will begin to happen. Many people find that coffee keeps them awake. My aunt will find that she is incredibly sleepy about twenty minutes after taking hers. I hope she won't be so sleepy that she goes to sleep in the drawing-room. That's a disturbing thought, but I don't think she will, and even if she does, Mary will put her to bed. I

hope, though, that the silly girl will not leap to the conclusion
that her mistress is ill, and ring up that wretched fellow
Spencer!

No, on the whole I think I have worked it out all right. I
tried these Somnoquubes first of all in my soup. That was a
most unfortunate experiment! They began to work before I
had finished dinner! Really, I had the utmost difficulty in
keeping awake until the meal was over, and as for staying
and drinking coffee, I just couldn't do it. I should have gone
to sleep at once, and I was so afraid I might talk in my sleep.
Indeed, I have a very imperfect recollection of what I did say
towards the end of the meal. All I really know it that I just
managed to plead tiredness and a headache and escape to
bed. The next day I discovered that my aunt had thought I
was drunk. Indeed, she even routed round in my room and
discovered a little absinth which I had smuggled back with
great difficulty and proceeded to destroy it. If she thought I
drank that stuff regularly, she was quite wrong, for though
I tried hard, having heard such intriguing stories of its effects,
I found it, in fact, very nasty. But I don't want her routing
round in my room.

The next time I experimented with the Somnoquubes I
took a smaller quantity in my coffee. This time the experiment worked very well. It was rather unpleasant for me,
as I had to fight off sleep desperately in order to stay the
conventional time with my aunt, but I had the satisfaction
of knowing that the effect was to bring on a sleep which
seemed natural, and which was certainly overpowering. One
does sleep soundly after them.

Soon after taking her coffee then tonight, my aunt will have
dragged sleep-laden footsteps out of her ugly drawing-room
to her austerely bare, but still ugly, bedroom. And then she
will go to sleep, and she will not wake up easily. I have seen
to that. At Brynmawr there is no modern coffee-pot. My aunt
will not allow such new-fangled things in the house. The
coffee is always made in some ghastly archaic way by pouring
boiling water onto beans—and I really don't know if they're

ground or not—and then strained. It is rather a long process, and the established custom from time immemorial is that it is done in the morning for lunch and dinner. For dinner it is heated up again—a statement which surely proves the method a bad one. In the interval the coffee stands in a particular jug on a particular shelf. It would, at Brynmawr. It was therefore easy for me to go into the pantry when Mary was clearing away lunch and slip a delicious Somnoquube into the jug.

I only hope, by the way, that the reheating did not affect its properties! I wonder if it is boiled? I think not actually. In which case I expect it will be all right. I should have liked to have asked that medical paper, but one could hardly do that.

But after all, the action of the Somnoquube is only secondary, it is only to make assurance doubly sure. For the fire will start in my bedroom wardrobe. It will soon get a good hold there—I have seen to that—and it will spread to the rest of my room quickly, and to the wainscoting of the wall, and so to the passage and, when once the passage is alight, the way to and from my aunt's bedroom next door will be cut off. The hall at Brynmawr, you see, is a large open one going up to the roof—with the result that the house is always cold in the winter. The stairs go up from it with the not very broad carpet that my aunt was so facetious about, and at the top a passage-way, divided from the hall only by a balustrade, leads along past my bedroom to my aunt's room over the drawing-room. The rooms nearer the top of the stairs are spare rooms, and there is also a passage leading to the servants' quarters and the attic—another unpleasant memory.

When, therefore, the passage outside my bedroom is burning well—and nobody will notice the fire till then—the servants will not be able to get to my aunt's room, and my aunt will be sleeping soundly. It will be a painless end. These old wooden houses burn so easily. It is dangerous to install electric light. Were not—oh, brilliant thought!—the lights fused only a week or so before? And I shall be miles away.

In fact I am miles away finishing writing these notes. In another forty-seven minutes the fire will start. I wonder how the news will be conveyed to me?

6

The next morning was dull and gray. As I had sat up a good while writing this diary, I was rather tired and sleepy. I should have very much liked to have had breakfast in bed and spent the morning resting for, apart from the shortage of sleep, I expected to have a very busy day in front of me.

But this was impossible. To begin with, though Guy is sympathetic and is able to see what true hospitality is, his family are a little disapproving. Though less Spartan than my aunt, I know that nevertheless he has his difficulties with them which I have no desire to increase—and breakfast in bed is always unpopular. Besides, I must appear completely natural, not a very easy thing to do when you are overtired and expecting peculiar news at any moment. Accordingly, I was just about the normal amount late for breakfast.

All the while I was dressing I expected a telegram; during breakfast I thought it must come—and nothing happened. We started to spend the morning examining some fittings Guy has added to his Bentley and chatting about the latest ideas in gears. I must admit I found it very hard to concentrate. All the time I had one eye on the drive up which, sooner or later, the telegraph boy, I felt, must come. And still he didn't.

And then an awful thought occurred to me. Supposing, after all, nothing happened? Supposing that by some incredible piece of bad luck something went wrong with my machinery, what would happen then? Well, in all probability, nothing would happen. I reassured myself. If nothing happened, nothing would happen. There was no real reason why anyone should go to my wardrobe, and if they did they would find it locked. It was a very stout lock in a well-made, substantial, mid-Victorian piece of furniture. It was unlikely that my aunt would have it broken open. There would be nothing to excite her curiosity sufficiently to overcome her dislike of damaging things. Her sense of economy would prevent her finding me out. Still, perhaps, it would be as well if nothing was heard by this evening, to drop her a line saying that I found I had accidentally taken the key of the wardrobe with me. I didn't usually worry to tell her that I had arrived safely and she would think it a bit odd, but it would save discovery and I could make my plans anew.

Yet, somehow, there kept creeping into my mind a picture of my aunt forcing open that wardrobe, of her discovering my arrangements, and then how could I explain them away? However, it's all right. I am writing these notes just before I return from Guy's simply because I should like to keep a record, though I have put it baldly and shortly, of the suspense I lived through this morning. Now that I know that there is no reason to worry, I cannot recapture the mood of alternating terror and confidence; besides, I do not wish to waste much time. I am anxious—for the first time in my life —to get back to Brynmawr. I am going to go directly after lunch which will be ready now at any moment. They have put it forward as much as they can so that I may get off.

But I have let my pen run away with me (an absurd phrase, by the way; pens do not run, but let that be), and have not recorded the contents of the telegram. It was very short and not very informative. It simply said: "Return at once. Spencer."

I am sorry Spencer signed it. I have no desire that he should poke his ugly face into the matter, but I suppose Cook or Mary would call him in to see what ought to be done. I hope, by the way, that they are unhurt; although I have some scores to settle with Cook, I do not bear malice against her to that extent. I wonder how they got hold of Spencer, for of course the telephone would be destroyed, but perhaps they managed to make a call to the Fire Brigade just before. Not that that would do any good. It takes many hours

to collect the Llwll brigade, I believe, since in the day time
the horses are out ploughing, and at night they have to send
round a man on a bicycle to wake the men up. But still, it
would start a rumor, and probably old Spencer would think
it necessary to go and see what had happened.

Ah, lunch is ready. I wonder where, and in what circumstances, I shall continue this!

I shall not forget that journey back in a hurry. As I left
Guy's the sun broke through the clouds, an omen of good
significance, I felt. I could almost have cheered, but fortunately I remembered that I must adopt a rather solemn,
worried demeanor. A telegram such as that usually means
"bad news"; at the same time I must remember that I could
have, in theory, no knowledge of what the bad news was
about. Oh, it was difficult to keep up that pose! I was glad
when I was clear of Guy's; another hour there and I believe
that I should have committed the indiscretion of letting him
into my confidence, and in view of the facts, loyal though
Guy is, that would have been a very definite mistake.

I literally sang as the good English roads passed beneath
me. The sun shone, La Joyeuse purred happily away, the
world was mine to do what I liked with. "Freedom, freedom,"
I exclaimed; "at last you are really mine!"

At that moment a little incident occurred which I ought to
have realized was more definitely an omen. One is not free
in this wretched country, ever. I was stopped by a police-
man who maintained that I was "driving to the danger."

"To the danger of what, Constable? Those sheep?"

"Partly, sir, and partly of the man with the sheep."

This was tiresome. I did not want my license endorsed
again. I tried, therefore, to bring diplomacy to my rescue. I
apologized to the representative of Bumdlebom and showed
him Spencer's telegram.

"I'm afraid that made me hurry. It's made me rather
anxious." At the same time I tried to slip half a crown into his

hand. Apparently this was not enough. The ridiculous fellow even looked insulted.

"No doubt, sir, the fact may be taken as a mitigating circumstance, but I shouldn't mention that!"

He pointed angrily to the hand that held the proffered coin, and proceeded to waste five minutes in taking my number. If the police would spend less time using long words like "mitigating circumstances" and get on with their job quicker, unfortunate motorists would have less time to make up. Meanwhile the sheep driver arrived and began to curse me in broad Salopian. Why *are* sheep allowed on the roads? I shall have *un mauvais quart d'heure* before the Abercwm bench. I only hope they don't take my license away.

It was some time before I regained my equanimity, and by then I had got on to the winding, badly repaired roads of Cwm. It was quite late in the afternoon before I crossed the bridge over the Brynmawr brook, and the afternoon sun was throwing the shadows of the trees right across the dingle. As I came up the hill the sun was straight in my eyes; I couldn't really see Brynmawr.

Of course, as a matter of fact, I didn't ever really expect to see Brynmawr again. I naturally assumed that the house would be entirely burnt to the ground. A few blackened walls, perhaps, at most a shell, but probably nothing, just a pile of ashes was all I expected to see. I mention this in detail because it explains what happened.

As I got into a patch of shade, the identical point at which I had contemplated placing an obstacle for my aunt to run into, I was able to see the house. And then I got a shock. The house was still standing apparently intact! For a moment my brain reeled and I drove a short way purely by instinct. Suddenly I was aware of the figure of my aunt standing on the road, straight in front of my car, looking exactly as she had always done in her lifetime.

Now I was quite convinced then that she must be dead. What else could Spencer's telegram mean? With an absolute wave of horror, I realized that my aunt's figure was standing at the identical spot where her car had left the road that afternoon a few weeks before. The conclusion seemed obvious to anyone as superstitious as I am. My aunt would always haunt that particular point on the road. Her spirit would try to cause me to make some error in driving, would try to force me to my destruction. That would be just like my aunt! But I made up my mind to show this ghost once and for all that I would not be intimidated. If I were not in the habit of using a very efficient Essence of Flowers, my hair would have stood on end, but as it was, with a curious tingling feeling in my scalp, I set my teeth, put my foot on the accelerator, and drove straight at this ghost.

With a startled scream the figure leapt to the side of the road, and catching one foot on the warning white stone by the side of the road, toppled over onto the ground. It was not until I was almost at the gate of the back yard that it occurred to me that this was very curious conduct for a ghost. After all, whatever you may say about spirits from the other world, they do not trip over stones. They glide through them. Nor for that matter do they worry to get out of the way of motor-cars. I put La Joyeuse into reverse and glided quietly and quickly back to the spot, just as the apparition collected itself and got onto the road again. Once more the figure hopped off the road; I only just missed it.

"Really, Edward," came my aunt's voice, quite unmistakably natural and lifelike, "you're becoming crude in your methods. And as for coming back again—well."

I had been through enough. I was tired and distracted, and I had just had a very terrible fright. I could only sit, I fear, with my mouth open, and gaze at my aunt. For it was my aunt. There was no mistaking it. That astounding woman was absolutely alive and well, and apparently quite convinced that I had just tried to run over her and, having failed, had tried again. In all the circumstances it was almost comic, but it was also very serious. For the one thing I had been anxious to avoid was that she should have any suspicion, and now, of course, she would have, as a result of a pure, unpremeditated and unintended accident which had had no effect whatever. It really was cruel!

My aunt's voice went on: "Damn it, Edward!" (I dislike women swearing) "I believe I've sprained my ankle." She hobbled up and down the road, testing it out, and eventually stopped by the side of La Joyeuse from which I had got out to make sure it was really her. Something, however, appeared to be interesting her in the car, for she examined the contents very carefully. "Three suit-cases, a portmanteau, which you told me once you wouldn't be seen dead with, a Gladstone bag—incidentally mine, my dear Edward—which I never expected to see you use. How long did you intend to stay with that Mr. Innes?"

"I wasn't quite sure. And one does want such a lot of variety in one's clothes there. They" (I slightly accentuated the pronoun) "provide so many different occupations for their guests. And everyone there is always well turned out."

My aunt continued to rummage in the car. "No doubt that's why you took your top hat?"

"Well, Guy told me there might be a local wedding while I was there." Rather a brilliant improvisation, I feel.

"Yes. They're often got up on the spur of the moment. Yes, yes. However, it's always well to be prepared. So you took your bowler in case they suddenly took you up to London, and your soft hat, of course, and your black velour one—I never know what the occasion is that you wear that thing, either in London or the country—and that horrible loud cap you drive in—and that old Panama. I hope you didn't wear that amongst the very-well-turned-out people, Edward" (she mimicked my voice—impertinent woman), "it's rather shabby, and your umbrella, and your malacca cane—you *were* prepared for every emergency." She paused and moved one or two things about. "But I never knew you had a straw boater, Edward dear."

I put a good face on it. "I bought it on the way there. In Shrewsbury. Oh, yes, it's a London make. I wouldn't take anything with a country name on it, of course. Servants are such snobs—"

"Servants, dear." My aunt must needs interrupt.

"Servants. They're getting quite fashionable now—straw hats, I mean," I added in reply to my aunt's raised eyebrows. "But don't call them 'straw boaters' please, Aunt Mildred."

"Very well, dear," said my aunt, with suspicious meekness. She turned away from the car. "Well, I can see there's no room in it for you to take me down to Llwll. Besides, I'm not quite sure I trust your driving after the way you drove just now. Anyhow, I think it'll do my ankle good to walk on it." She started off down the road. "Good-bye for the present, dear."

I could bear it no longer. "What's this telegram of Spencer's mean, Aunt Mildred?"

"Tell you later, dear." My aunt was rapidly going off down the road. "Must hurry now. You should have asked me before and not kept me waiting while you explained about not calling them straw boaters. Back for dinner." My aunt waved her stick cheerily as she disappeared round the corner—ungrammatical, horrid, sneering, uncouth, imperious woman!

I hurried La Joyeuse into the garage and, leaving my luggage in it, rushed up to my room. The wardrobe had completely disappeared, a large patch of the carpet was burnt, there were marks of fire on the wall. I tried to remember what had been there. Very much to my annoyance I remembered that there had been a bookcase by the side of the wardrobe, with some of my not most precious, but still cherished, books, and this had completely disappeared.

The fire, then, had started. It had burnt the wardrobe. Well, there was nothing of value in that. It had destroyed some of my books. That was sad, but not very material. My carpet was ruined. I doubt if I shall ever exactly get that shade again. But that was all. Nothing very material, providing—There is the catch. How was it put out, and what did my aunt suspect was the cause of the fire? It was most un-

fortunate that she had examined the luggage in my car.
I had taken everything I could get in, but I really think it
would not have been noticeable but for that unlucky last
straw of the straw hat which I genuinely had bought on the
way. And I ought to have sacrificed my top hat; but I had
better write to Guy and get him to confirm the possibility of
a hypothetical wedding. I needn't explain it all to him, but
I could trust him to back me up if I told him what was
wanted, without knowing all the circumstances.

But there is one phrase of my aunt's I do not like: "You're
becoming crude in your methods." "Becoming . . . methods."
Now what exactly did she mean? Am I to imply from that
all the unpleasant possibilities that one might deduce, or
was it just chance? Well, my aunt will be back soon from
Llwll, and then presumably I shall know. I have never found
it difficult, at any rate, to read every thought in my aunt's
head.

7

My aunt is becoming very mysterious. She simply will not
explain. Indeed, she treats the whole matter as if there were
nothing to explain. Apparently she seems to think that, as my
wardrobe had been burnt, it was quite natural that she
should summon me back. As for why Spencer sent the wire,
or why his name was at the foot of it, she has given absolutely
no hint at all as yet. In some ways I should be content to
leave things just as they are, and let the incident slip from
her mind; but there are two reasons against this. First of all,
would it be entirely natural to accept the whole thing as a
matter of course? Supposing that the fire was quite accidental,
shouldn't I be asking all sorts of questions, making all sorts
of fuss? I think I should, and would like to start making the
fuss that I should be likely to make, only I am not quite
sure how I should tackle it. In short, I'm a bit afraid of
overacting.

The second point, which worries me much more, is my

aunt's almost unnatural avoidance of the subject. Usually if she has a grievance, there is no mistaking it. There is no lack of directness, no finesse about my aunt at all. She says what she wishes to say like the proverbial bull in a china shop. She approaches those difficult situations where angels might well fear to tread, with the delicacy and deliberateness of a steam-roller. Poor Aunt Mildred. She has little *savoir-faire*—normally.

But it is not so certain that she is not being rather diplomatic at the present moment. She is lying so miraculously low, and keeping so unnaturally quiet, that I am in danger of having not the worst of the argument—there is no argument—but the worst of the silence. And I really feel as if soon I shall say something indiscreet!

Let me record the few conversations we have had on the subject.

The first one was at dinner on the night I came back. I opened by hoping she had enjoyed her walk into Llwll. Rather a futile remark, I must admit, as she always does, and I never do, and anyhow she must have known I was quite indifferent as to whether she did or not. On the whole, I must admit I rather deserved the retort I got—the opening was too easy.

"Yes, dear, thank you, despite my ankle."

I ignored that. "You were going to tell me why you, or rather why Dr. Spencer, sent that wire for me to come back."

My aunt raised her eyebrows. "Haven't you been upstairs?"

"Yes, Aunt. Having dressed. I gather there was a fire in my room. But why bring me back for that?"

A complete silence reigned. My aunt gazed at a moderate little picture, an ancestress of ours with a blue hat with a gray feather in it, powdered hair, and a quite pleasant smile. On the wall opposite me was a less attractive canvas. It represented some Scriptural character. Jacob, I think, meeting a young woman, Rebecca, I believe, at a well. The well is surrounded by dark smudges which faintly resemble oak trees with luxuriant foliage, unlikely, I should imagine, in Palestine. Jacob is making the sort of bow practised at the

Court of Louis-Quatorze, and the young woman is simpering abominably. Behind Jacob is his faithful camel—a starved-looking animal with a sly smile. The camel appears to be the only person with an idea in his head, which is to take a large mouthful out of the dirty and inadequate brown cloak which Jacob has hitched round him. After which, as Jacob wears apparently nothing else, there will, I imagine, be a scene. I have always hated that picture since my earliest days. My grandfather took it over, I have been told, for a bad debt. It must have been a very bad debt, and on the whole I think that housing the atrocity increased, rather than diminished it, but there it remains. "It isn't very beautiful, but it always has hung there, dear," was my aunt's inevitable reply when I did once venture to protest.

After gazing at this masterpiece for some minutes I repeated my question. There was quite a perceptible pause before my aunt deigned to reply.

"The Insurance, dear; but as you took everything away with you, you won't, of course, put in a claim."

"But surely that could have waited?"

Another silence ensued. At any moment the camel would snatch those rags. I've been waiting for it, fascinated, for years.

"Could you, dear?"

Now I should like to be certain if my aunt said "Could you" or "Could it." "It" would be more reasonable but "you" is terribly near true, when I remember the state of suspense I was in at Guy's. I shouldn't like to think that had occurred to my aunt's mind. Surely she must have said "it," and yet I could have sworn she said "you."

The next morning I opened the subject again. My aunt had started the conversation by saying she felt better.

"The night before last, you know, Edward, I felt so sleepy after drinking my coffee, just like you did the other night, you remember. The coffee tasted a bit funny, too." I looked sharply at her, but her expression was blandly unconscious. "And then, of course, the fire kept me awake."

"I wish you'd tell me what happened, Aunt."

"But there's nothing to tell you, Edward. The wardrobe caught fire, and then the bookcase, and then I put it out—with a fire extinguisher."

"I never knew we had a fire extinguisher in the house—except on the cars."

"No, we usen't to. Wasn't it lucky, I'd just got one in. Something I read made me think of it."

"In the paper, Aunt Mildred?"

"Yes, or was it a magazine, or a book? Anyhow it was a good thing I had one. The wardrobe burnt tremendously quickly. Finished, dear?" My aunt prepared to rush off on her busy pursuit of nothing.

"Just finished. I shall see about the claim on the Insurance Company this morning, I think."

"Better not, Edward. There was nothing in the wardrobe. The books are not covered by the policy, and the carpet is really mine, though I know you think it's yours. So on the whole, Edward, better not claim, I think. Don't you?"

She departed, carrying a tray, and shutting the door by winding her toe round it as she went—two odious habits. The servants are underworked without her helping them, and the door trick is definitely vulgar.

Really, though, I am getting a little nervous. Is it possible that there is any significance to be attached to her remarks? Of course I don't intend to claim—I merely thought it would seem unnatural if I didn't pretend to—but as a matter of fact, Insurance Companies do ask such awkward questions, and I had no desire to have them prying round. But I don't like to think that my aunt knows that I "had better not." Is it possible she suspects something?

I wish I could get a more coherent account from her, or from Cook, or from Mary, of what happened; but both Cook and Mary just look blank and ignorant. They maintain they slept through whatever did happen, and my aunt is evasive. I rather gather that those cubes tasted the coffee—I can only say they didn't taste mine—and consequently my aunt drank only a little of it. So she got sleepy, and then the drowsiness passed off, leaving her probably even more wide awake than usual. With the result, I suppose, that the first signs of fire woke her, or roused her, as she tossed about restlessly. That would be just about when the wardrobe was well ablaze; and then she put it out with these unlucky extinguishers. I wonder where and what she read which made her go to that unwonted extravagance. Something, I suppose, about a country house being burnt down. Good thing it wasn't this diary she read! That really is an amazing thought! I laugh as I write it. But what bad luck she had got them just in time, and yet not so very unlucky, because there would have been little point in burning down the house while she was awake. No, it was those rotten Somnoquubes that let me down. But yet I can't understand that. I *know* they're effective, and I swear they don't taste. It's rather worrying. I suppose she doesn't know more than she pretends? Life would be intolerable if she did.

I have just made one more try to find out more. I asked her again why Spencer signed the wire.

"Oh, he was going into Llwll, so I asked him to do it."

"For you? I should have thought he'd have added your name."

"Not if *he* sent it, Edward dear." Her voice seemed to pity my ignorance and lack of decent feeling. "He's a very honorable man, you know, and would never sign anyone else's name."

"I'm not accusing him of forgery, my dear Aunt Mildred, but I couldn't make it out. As a matter of fact, I think it was very inconsiderate of him. I feared that something had happened to you."

"Feared? and what exactly did you think had happened? Are you sure it was 'feared,' Edward?"

Her eyes seemed to bore into my brain. For a second the whole room whirled round me. Then the strange look, if it had ever been there, died out of my aunt's eyes. Her red face ceased to peer into mine, and instead of seeming to be so close to mine that she could see into my very brain, I was able to see that it was the normal distance off and really rather expressionless.

"Why, what I mean is, what should you be frightened of? I'm very well capable of taking care of myself, Edward."

I do not for a moment doubt it. In fact I have very good proof that she is capable of doing so. I might even go so far as to say that ever since I was born she has spent her time demonstrating her complete ability to look after herself—if not after me. But all the same I wish I was quite sure which of her two sentences she really did mean. "Are you sure it was 'feared,' Edward? Why, what I mean is, what should you be frightened of?" I think I have her words right, but it makes a great deal of difference whether her real thoughts came first, and the second half was a disguise; or whether the first half was an accidental slip, a stronger phrase than she intended, and the second really genuinely explanatory. I cannot decide which of the two views is the right one.

But I am certain of one thing. I have been reading over these conversations and considering them word by word, and I now see clearly that my aunt's conduct is highly suspicious. I must watch her movements very carefully.

4: *In a Garden Growing*

I AM now quite sure I am right. My aunt is an extremely deceitful woman. She must, I suppose, for years past have been in the habit of concealing her feelings towards me. At any rate, it is quite certain that she suspects very much more than she says of what has been happening. I cannot think exactly what she bases her suspicions on; in fact, I do not even know quite what she thinks, but I am sure she has jumped to conclusions, and unfortunately to right conclusions. Of course she is practically incapable of carrying out a logical piece of thought, but she does guess unpleasantly well.

I can well understand that the burning of that wardrobe must have seemed odd. In fact, the more I look back on that, the more I blush about it. It all comes of taking as accurate the half-baked ideas of a man like Jack Spencer. Just because he has a sort of a commission in an infantry battalion, he must needs think that he knows everything about work more properly done by the Engineers. Besides, all the Spencers are fools. And that job was one which, if it did not succeed, was bound to look curious. I ought to have made certain of it; that was my mistake, of course, but I cannot for the life of me see how I could have made sure, unless I had covered the room with petrol, and that would have been stupid because it would have smelt so.

However, even if that business did look curious, I still think that a really nice-minded woman would have given the thing the benefit of the doubt, and assumed that it was what it appeared to be—an accident—and that is the exact word that my aunt used today, obviously satirically about,

not only that, but apparently about her smash in her car;
and whatever she may say, that was an accident in a sense,
and why she should imagine that it wasn't, I cannot think.
All of which merely goes to show that my aunt has a very
unpleasant mind. But let me jot down the incident.

I am, of course, not going to admit defeat. I am already
casting round in my mind for a way to ensure success, and
with that end in view I was trying to get information this
morning from the *Encyclopedia Britannica*. Rather a tiresome work, I find it; it seems to be full of information, but
almost never to have the exact answer to the question one is
propounding. However, I was using it for want of anything
better when I was startled by hearing my aunt's unpleasant
harsh voice just behind me.

"The pursuit of knowledge and Edward Powell in con-
junction. Gracious me, how unexpected. Surely that can teach
you nothing, my dear Edward. It's the *Encyclopedia Britannica*, and surely nothing British is of interest to you, you're far
above that," and thereupon she started whistling, if you
please, an infuriating tune from that tawdry man, Gilbert
and Sullivan, about "the idiot who praises in a sentimental
tone every century but this and every country but his own,"
or some such words, I don't worry to know such trash. My
aunt imagines it to be a certain method of annoying me—
and, to be honest, she is not far wrong! So very foolish.

I could not help an involuntary movement of my hands to
my ears, but I took very good care to close the volume
quickly.

"Spare us, *please,* Aunt Mildred, so very out of tune, and
whistling!"

"I'm glad you know the tune, and the sentiment, dear."

"I managed to recognize it. You generally whistle it the
same way, though I doubt if it's the way the composer meant."

"Never mind what the composer meant, Edward dear. I
don't think you could ever understand either of them. But
what are you so absorbed in in the *Encyclopedia?*"

Now I could not possibly tell her exactly what I had been

looking up, and unfortunately I had no ready reply prepared in advance. The situation was really rather difficult. However, if my aunt must insinuate portions of the *Mikado,* why shouldn't I? With what I trust was a peculiarly exasperating smile I hummed gently:

> *"Tit-willow, Tit-willow, Tit-willow."*

The devil may quote Gilbert—my aunt's second Bible almost—for his purpose! The quotation game seemed to amuse her.

> *"This haughty youth*
> *He speaks the truth*
> *Whenever he finds it pays"*

she retorted, and under the cover of that I managed to get the volume back onto the shelf and change the subject. I hoped that I had heard the end of it, but unfortunately that flattering unction was laid to my soul too soon. When I said good night to my aunt this evening, she raised the point once more.

"I didn't insist this morning in knowing exactly what you were looking up. I fancy, Edward, you would have found it difficult to answer. Now, I only want to say one thing, I shall not allow any more"—there seemed to be a slight pause, and just sufficient emphasis to justify my use of the word "satirical"—"any more accidents, Edward. If I find another happens, I shall have to take action. And when I say I am going to take action, Edward, you know very well that I do, and I don't generally give previous notice about it. So, for the first and last time, Edward, no more accidents."

I wouldn't allow her, of course, to get away with that unchecked.

"Oh, Aunt, I'm so glad you're going to take some driving lessons."

"Don't be silly, Edward." My aunt really did seem to be annoyed. I knew that was a soft spot of hers, for in her heart

of hearts I think she knows she is a bad driver. "Do not bo
silly in any way, Edward."

I looked at her quite steadily.

"No, Aunt, I shan't, good night." And I don't intend to be
silly. I mean to be completely successful. For I have no
illusions; if my aunt says she will take action, she will, and
it will be very unpleasant action too. In fact I am amazed
at the courage I show in staying here after what has happened.
I really think that, if my plans were to miscarry again, there
would be nothing left for me but flight. Only I don't know
where to fly to. If only I did!

I am not sure, looking back on it, that I was quite wise to
bring in the car. Supposing my aunt was putting me through
a sort of third-degree method—the torture being merely
mental—and had deliberately suddenly said "accident" to
see what my reaction was. It was perhaps a mistake to have
fallen into the trap by saying "car," but she did say "accidents,"
not "accident." However, my next move is clear. If my aunt is
going to be so stupid as to be suspicious, her suspicions must
be lulled for ever. So far, I have been handicapped by a
foolish, sentimental desire to lull them painlessly, but if she
threatens "action," retaliation, it must be done at all costs,
even if the method is painful. I can imagine her quoting her
favorite author as to "something lingering with boiling oil"—
not that I intend to go so far as that. But she has taken the
gloves off now. There will be no rules for the future.

2

I have escaped for the moment from Brynmawr.

My real reason is that I wish to look up various books of
reference in peace and quiet and without the risk of being
disturbed by my aunt. I discovered her, by the way, diligently
searching through the *Encyclopedia,* despite her statement
that she did not insist on knowing what I was looking up, a
performance which I can barely call truthful. Of course I

had to make some excuse to get away from Cwm, but that was not difficult. I have always refused to employ a local dentist, and even my aunt cannot deny that one's teeth must be seen to occasionally; in fact, she is generally pressing me to go. Like so many people, she has Spartan, and doubtless correct, views about the necessity of other people going to dentists at frequent and regular intervals but, also like other people, she never puts them into practice herself.

I also added rather cleverly as a further excuse, that I needed to replace the clothes burnt in my wardrobe. I could not admire the way my aunt raised her eyebrows at this.

Accordingly, then, I am writing this seated in a rather old-fashioned, uncomfortable club I belong to. I can't think why I do. It really is entirely foreign to my nature, but apparently it was a wish of my mother's. She seemed to have an idea, so my aunt tells me, that the old fogeys who use this place will have a tendency to turn me into an old fogey of exactly the same deplorable pattern as themselves. How they will do it is as mysterious as the wish that they should do so. However, the wish was expressed, and my aunt has sternly fulfilled it—she would. She has paid my subscription every year and calls it, forsooth, a Christmas present—a mean way of getting out of it, to my mind, and so lacking in originality. However, it saves me from having to think much. I give her a French novel in return, pointing out that she will also improve her mind by my present to her. She seldom, however, reads it, and I seldom use the club. I have one advantage over her, though. I can read the novel, but she is prohibited from coming into the club.

Nevertheless, besides the fact that it sounds well to belong to it, there are moments when its peace is useful, and this is one of them. To be honest, I have not quite made up my mind as to the method I am going to try, and I want to think it out. So far, however, I have only got the general idea that some form of poison seems to be best. The difficulty, of course, is to find a poison which leaves no very obvious trace behind. If I could only be certain that nobody but old Spencer would make an examination, I should be comparatively happy, since, if I avoided the most obvious things, he would be sure to fail to find anything out. Another thing I want to find out is how you obtain it. That, of course, is going to be difficult. The whole idea may be impossible; still, I intend to investigate it. I have been looking round the almost incredible club library—the classical and religious rubbish there is in it is unbelievable—and I cannot find a good medical work on poisons, so I had better start with the article in the *Encyclopedia* I was glancing at when my aunt interrupted me.

Here, then, is the volume. Plan to Raym. Plants, Plumbing, Poetry. Here we are, Poison. Now let's see what we can find that's useful. On the whole, I think a few notes would be a good plan.

It starts with some talk about the law—a subject which I would prefer to leave out. "The sale of poisons to the public is carefully controlled by law, and the danger to human life from the indiscriminate sale of poisons by unqualified persons is thereby reduced." Now, how very surprising that is! and how very little it helps to know it!

Next there is some talk about powdered glass and metallic filings. Those are two good ideas to have down and find out a little more about. On the whole, though, rather too well known, too much of a *vieux jeu* for my taste, or my safety. "Poisoning may be accidental, suicidal, or homicidal. By far the commonest type is that due to accidental causes." Exactly. I wish I could make old Spencer read that and learn it by heart! But it is curious how this word "accident" keeps cropping up. I mustn't, of course, forget that this is to be an accident.

Now here's something useful in the very next sentence. "In spite of the precautions taken by the State in the sale of poisons, much too little care is taken by the public in the safeguarding of poisons in their possession, and these are commonly taken in mistake for other substances of harmless nature, or often an overdose is taken from pure carelessness.

Thus oxalic acid crystals when purchased in a paper packet may be transferred to a bottle or jar which is unlabelled, and then taken in mistake for Epsom salts, which they closely resemble."

I wonder if that could be worked. Probably, as I gather it from the passage I have copied out, I shouldn't be able to buy oxalic acid crystals, whatever they may be. However, I've made a note to see if one can buy them. Also to see if there is any simple way of making them. Probably not, and there is also the difficulty that my aunt does not, so far as I know, ever take Epsom salts—which I must admit is a drawback.

However, to return to our *Encyclopedia.* Corrosive sublimate taken as Blaud's pills. Somehow, that doesn't appeal to me, though I should think it would come into the category of "something lingering with boiling oil in it." "Usually the quantity of poison taken bears a relation to the effects produced"—well, so one would think. Oh, I see, if you take too much of some things you are sick before you are poisoned, and oxalic acid is one of them. Really, this man seems to have been considering the difficulties very intelligently. I wonder if he had an aunt?

Habit, idiosyncrasy. I can't pretend my aunt ever had any tendency to take drugs, and as for idiosyncrasy, well, my aunt is full of them, but I don't know her idiosyncrasies as regards aceto-salicylic acids unfortunately, and I don't quite see how I can find out. Age, state of health, none of this seems to apply. Condition and mode of administration. Now that's exactly what I want to be instructed in. Blessings on the fellow. I hope his paragraph is useful. It's all too short—and dash it, it's of very little practical use.

From it, however, there are a few useful points to note down. Poisons are more effective when swallowed as a liquid, more rapid when taken before meals, more powerful when administered subcutaneously or intravenously. That's all very well, but I can hardly pretend to inoculate my aunt, puncturing her skin or her veins which I suppose is what is meant.

Unless I could arrange a poisoned rusty nail? That's one to bear in mind. I'll put that down in my list of possibles. It would be nearer to being possible if I knew what sort of poison one used.

To continue, Diagnosis and Treatment. That's Spencer's business. Characteristics. This needs careful reading . . . Corrosive, Irritant, Systematic, Gaseous Poisons, Poisonous Foods. There may be some idea to be picked up from the last heading, which includes mushrooms and shellfish. It would be poetic justice if mushrooms could be brought in, for both Spencer and my aunt dared to doubt my word as to the mushroom I thought I saw in the meadow in front of Brynmawr just before poor So-so was so foully murdered.

Corrosive poisons. These seem very unpleasant, even worse than I care to contemplate, and, moreover, apparently very easily detected, and even possibly curable. That won't do. There must be no mistake this time; one of the remedies is so simple a thing as white of egg, and that could be got in any quantity at Brynmawr without difficulty. I must try and find something requiring a more obscure antidote.

Ammonia seems to be a possibility. One could, I suppose, get hold of it fairly easily; but I see one has to get a specially strong solution, which might be difficult, even though one drachm has been sufficient to cause death, and so probably two would be enough. I wonder, by the way, exactly how much a drachm is? But anyhow, you can't help noticing the smell. It isn't as if I was going to have the opportunity of forcibly feeding my aunt. However, that can go down amongst the possibles.

Here, I think, is another. "Carbolic acid is commonly used as a disinfectant for domestic purposes. Allied preparations such as creosote, creosol, have a similar poisonous effect." (I could easily get hold of creosol, and then there's Jeyes, I wonder if that's got carbolic acid in it?) "Carbolic acid is one of the poisons most frequently used by suicides," goes on my valuable if unconscious colleague. Now I wonder if I could make it look like suicide? On the whole I think not.

That means inquiry; besides, my aunt has no reasons in the world to do such a thing, unless—ironic thought—you call me one! "And owing to its common use for domestic purposes accidental poisoning by it often occurs." Excellent! But how can anybody drink enough carbolic acid to poison themselves without noticing the taste? Surely you'd be bound to spot it, even in a cocktail, and I've had one of those so badly made that it tasted pretty nearly as nasty.

One of these drachm things, I see, has caused death in twelve hours. Too slow. Even old Spencer might effect a cure in that time, especially as, since it is a common poison, he might perhaps know something about curing it. I shan't even put it down.

And now for the Irritant poisons. "Oxalic acid is commonly used for cleaning straw hats, removing ink stains, cleaning brasses, &c. It is frequently the cause of accidental and suicidal poisoning." Then I presume that, after all, it cannot be so difficult to get. Yes, and my aunt was very sarcastic about my straw hat; straw boater, was her offensive phrase. Underline oxalic acid.

"Unless immediate treatment is adopted collapse speedily occurs . . . death is likely to occur rapidly, e.g. within an hour, but it may be delayed." Undoubtedly make full inquiries. And I shall not give the antidote, a pint of lime water made into a thin cream with an ounce of chalk. It sounds disgusting.

Arsenic. No; too much is known about arsenic. I am wise enough not even to read the paragraph through. "Prussic acid . . . is met with in commerce only in a dilute state." Still it is met with. "Less than a teaspoonful of the two per cent acid has caused death. The symptoms of prussic-acid poisoning set in with great rapidity, and in consequence the onset of the symptoms is reckoned by seconds rather than minutes." This sounds promising. I don't really like the idea of watching a slow process. Moreover, I see that "other soluble cyanides, more especially cyanide of potassium, a salt largely used in photography, are equally poisonous with hydrocyanic acid." That means it's possible to get it. I think I had better put that on my list. I'll just read the paragraph through again.

No, I've struck it out. "The lightning-like character of the illness, and the speedy death of the patient, coupled with the peculiar odour of the acid, seldom leave any doubt as to the nature of the death." That won't do at all—obviously. Careful, now. Be steady. *Keep your head.*

What's this? "Aconite poisoning. The ordinary aconite, wolfsbane, or monkshood, and an alkaloid extracted from it, aconitine, are perhaps the most deadly of known poisons. One-sixteenth of a grain of aconitine has proved fatal to a man"—and therefore, I suppose, to a woman, but here we have the real point. "The root of aconite has been eaten in mistake for that of horseradish."

Splendid and excellent. That awful Sunday dinner at Brynmawr nearly always consists of roast beef, and my aunt always eats plenty of horseradish sauce, which I don't touch—I never have. There can be no argument about it. Mary could bear out that statement. If I could substitute the aconite roots for the horseradish ones the trick would be done. They must be sufficiently alike if the mistake has been made before, for Cook not to notice it. By the way, I wonder if Cook or Mary eat horseradish sauce? Probably there will be some disturbance before they start their dinner. It depends how quickly the thing acts. I hope there will be, but Cook deserves anything she gets, and as for that kitchen-maid, she really doesn't count. She's barely human. Mary. Well, Mary has betrayed me. Still, on the whole, I hope they won't have time to start on it.

The next point, then, is to find out all about aconite. As a matter of fact, I don't even know what it looks like, but with any luck I can find something out about it here. For the moment I think I have done enough and can call it a day. I hope this Club can provide me with a decent lunch; I feel I have deserved it after this very energetic morning.

3

Lunch was quite pleasant, even if the company of old fogeys who sit around look a bit depressing. They all have heavy, expensive-looking faces and drink quantities of vintage port to wash down heavy beef-and-mutton sort of meals. In fact, one near me I should describe in a paraphrase of the public-house offer as the sort of man who habitually lunched off two cuts off the joint and one veg. I listened to some of his conversation. He seemed to have only one thought, namely, when would the Stilton be fit to eat? So far, he complained, it was chalky and quite unripe.

I chose my own lunch with more care and, I hope, a prettier taste. The dressed crab was excellent, and so was the *perdreau périgourdin.* I added an *omelette espagnole* and some very drinkable claret to accompany it. Rather a larger lunch than I usually have, but I must admit I was hungry— the efforts of the morning, I suppose. After a short rest I walked up Regent Street to look at the shops chiefly. My ideas may be a little out of date, I feel, after rusticating for so long. I am glad to notice that the fashion of putting stereo-typed labels on clothes, as if they were vegetables, is depart-ing. It used always to be "The latest," "As worn," "This season's," or at the most dashing "Very chic." Now, however, I found a shop which has really broken away from that sort of thing. "Too, too divine," "Dev'lish" are its allurements. The sort of things one might say. "Simply scrumptious" I thought was perhaps too slangy, especially as the garment, a brown jumper, seemed to me to be a very ordinary, rather drab affair. "Stupendously stunning," however, was the *mot juste* for an orange slashed with gray tweed coat, with large mother-of-pearl buttons, and the suspicion of a fur collar. I could not help laughing as I wondered what my aunt would look like in it. The effect would be enough to knock anyone down. But then my aunt's clothes usually are a source of amusement, not only to me, but I believe to most other people. I wish that shop sold men's clothes. I feel sure they would have something that would appeal to me.

However, I had a little experimental work to do. I turned into a large chemist's. At least, they used to be chemists, but really, nowadays, they seem to be everything else as well. My idea was simply to find out if I could buy any oxalic acid crystals. Not that I have made up my mind to use them, but knowledge is always power, as some platitudinous poet remarked.

Now what followed was really curious, and I put it down just to remind myself of one of the few moments of real weakness I have ever had. I sidled in over a pavement curiously inlaid with drawings of tooth-brushes and hair-brushes, and even sponges and combs—very modern, but rather odd, and finally made my way towards a jade-green, octagonal counter displaying myriads of bath salts piled up in charming array with most seductive wrappers. There were several kinds I was sure I should like—they were shaded so delicately and so alluringly named—only my aunt makes such a fuss over the delicate perfume. I turned away reluctantly and not quite sure which way to go. Immediately one of these all too efficient shop-walkers swept down on me, making me feel about twelve.

"Can I assist you, sir? What department do you require?"

Why couldn't the fellow say "want"? However, I found it equally impossible to say "The poison department," and for some absurd reason I found I could not say "I want to buy some oxalic acid crystals."

The fellow looked as if he could see right through me, and —stupid though it sounds—I completely lost my head and said the first thing that came into my mind. "I—er—want—er —some—er—Christmas cards," was my idiotic reply.

"Certainly, sir, on the second floor, sir. They will direct you there, sir. You will pardon my saying so, sir, but your forethought in seeing to the matter so early—it is only September, sir—is very wise, sir, I am sure, sir. But I rather wonder, sir, if our department will have their full stock yet, sir. This way, sir. The lift will take you." And with that he pushed me, rather than ushered me, into a lift already full of women with faces like Brussels sprouts, and snapped "Christmas cards" to the lift-boy, who, for the moment, to judge by the surprise on his face, clearly thought that this was an ejaculation, startling in one so decorous. The Brussels-sprout-faced women all sniffed, and one, with more truth than she knew, murmured audibly, "I don't believe it."

I crawled out of the place as wise as when I went in, and considerably shaken, with a most ridiculous picture of a robin trying to eat a very prickly holly leaf in my pocket.

On the way back I came across another branch—slightly less grandiloquent in appearance. This time I rushed in, and, addressing a pale-faced be-spectacled youth, exclaimed in one breath:

"Can—I—buy—some—oxalic—acid—crystals—please?"

The youth folded up a sheet of paper and looked at me disapprovingly. "One minute, sir, please. I'm serving this lady, now."

I was in such a state of nerves that I could have sworn she was one of the Brussels-sprout women from the lift, but really she couldn't be. All that sort of women are so alike, though, anyhow.

Eventually the youth turned to me. "Oxalic acid crystals, sir? You know it's a poison, sir?"

If he had only known how funny his question was, we should have been all square in knowledge. However, I kept my head.

"Of course."

The youth regarded me gravely. "Excuse me, sir, but for what purpose do you require them?"

"To clean my straw hat."

The youth was visibly startled by this rather unexpected reply. "Er—yes, sir, certainly, sir. So many gentlemen find it simpler to get their hatters to save them the trouble, but they are getting more fashionable, sir." He brightened visibly.

It was necessary to make an effort "I live in the depth of the country with no intelligent hatter within miles, and I find it inconvenient to come up to London every time I want my hat cleaned. If you wouldn't mind serving me—"

"Certainly, sir, I'll just call Mr. Marshbanks. Certain formalities, you know, sir, as it is a poison. Shan't keep you waiting a second. The register has to be signed, I believe, sir, Mr. Marshbanks knows all about it. Just a second, sir."

"Oh, if there's all that trouble, thank you, I won't worry. No doubt something else will be adequate for my purpose. I was told that was the best stuff, though."

"Just as you please, sir; but I really shouldn't have to keep you more than a minute. Ah, there *is* Mr. Marshbanks."

Mr. Marshbanks from a distance appeared to be the twin brother of the shop-walker up the road. The resemblance was so great that I accidentally exclaimed "Christmas cards" and then, turning back to the startled assistant, hurriedly refused to let him take any more trouble. The thing, I explained, was too trivial. I left the shop with an unpleasant feeling that I was an object of extreme suspicion to the pale-faced youth now talking rapidly to Mr. Marshbanks.

But nothing like so bad an object of suspicion as I should have been if I had been fool enough to sign that register with my own name and address, and then used the stuff successfully on my aunt. And as for giving a false name and address, it's awfully hard to think of one on the spur of the moment with any realism at all. Besides, they might have wanted to post it or to verify it or goodness knows what. Really, the laws of this country are positively ridiculous if you can't buy a few crystals to clean a straw hat without all this fuss and bother. I suppose it's Dora or some silly act like that. I should really like to go into Parliament just to pass one act, namely, to repeal all stupid, obsolete, vexatious, irritating, unnecessary, tyrannical and useless acts and all parts of all other acts which were stupid, obsolete, &c. The statute book would be quite considerably shorter.

Meanwhile the *Encyclopedia* has let me down. Oxalic acid

apparently can be made by oxidizing sugar with nitric acid—but the details of how to do so are not given. You can also start with sawdust made into a stiff paste with a mixture of strong caustic potash and soda solution, and heated in flat iron pans to 200–250 degrees—which is impossible, though it sounds a lovely mud-pie. Again you can, if you are able to, heat sodium in a current of carbon-dioxide to 360 degrees centigrade. Thank you so much. And again they go on to encourage one by talking of its similarity to Epsom salts, a very tiresome book. It will have to be aconites.

4

However, first catch your aconite, and then cook it.

"The aconite has a short, underground stem, from which dark-colored, tapering roots descend. The horseradish root is much longer than that of the aconite, and it is not tapering; its color is yellowish, and the top of the root has the remains of the leaves on it." On the whole I wish it was the other way round, since then one could take the root, shorten it, make it taper, add a little yellow paint and remove the leaves, but if I do that now, I'm merely making a piece of horseradish look like an aconite, making the sheep put on wolf's clothing —wolfsbane clothing, one might say. However, probably Cook won't know all that, though it would be just like that tiresome woman to say, "This doesn't look right somehow," and throw my possibly laboriously acquired aconite roots away.

But to continue. "The roots of aconitum ferox supply the famous Indian (Nepal) poison called bikh, bish, or nabee. It contains considerable quantities of the alkaloid pseuda-conitine which is the most deadly poison known." I pause to smile. "As garden plants the aconites are very ornamental, hardy perennials. They thrive well in any ordinary garden soil, and will grow beneath the shade of trees." Well, that ought to make it easy to grow them at Brynmawr. I wonder,

by the way, if I shall have to grow some from seed, or if I
can get some small plants? If it's seeds I may have to wait till
next spring before I sow them, and that will make a year in
all. Perhaps I can buy fully grown plants with luck. I suppose
I shall have to go one of these nursery gardeners. I hope
they aren't as particular about poisonous plants as chemists
are!

Still, however, I don't know what the things look like. The
Encyclopedia goes on to burble about veratryl-pseudaconine,
veratric acid, Japaconitine (obtained from the Japanese
aconites, known locally, but not by me, as "kuza-uza"), and
finally gets involved in japbenzaconine. It then remarks,
"Many species of aconite are cultivated in gardens, some
having blue, and others yellow flowers," from which, of
course, it will be quite easy to find it. Oh, yes. So have
pansies; and that's all that can be got from that except the
comforting statement that the only post-mortem sign is that
of asphyxia, not that it matters since, even if the cause is
discovered, the reason is going to be the carelessness of
Evans.

But I still have not caught my aconite.

As a reference library this club is sadly lacking. As I think
I said before, religion and the classics are here in quantities
—but who wants either? Except the solvers of those obscure
crossword puzzles by Torquemada. Poetry, Travel, Belles-
Lettres, History, Dictionaries all have their place in the notice
giving a guide to the method in which it is arranged, but
Botany does not seem to be a leading subject. However, by
the aid of a great deal of research in the most curious card-
index, I have amassed a short selection.

The Illustrated Dictionary of Gardening (an Encyclopedia
of Horticulture), bought in 1911 and written, I should think,
by Queen Victoria's grandmother.

Withering's *Botany* (1812).

London's *Encyclopedia of Plants* (1855).

The Latin Names of Common Plants, by a member of the
Club, I observe.

The English Flower Garden, 1st Edition, 1883, 6th Edition, 1898.

These five, so far as I can make out, complete the list. Whoever buys the books for this Club seems to be echoing Mr. Hardcastle. "I love everything that is old; old books, old wine, and even an old wife." I agree with Mrs. Hardcastle's disgusted reaction to the remark. How I hated that play when I had to read it as a holiday task!

The second and third of my selection of books can be discarded at once. They are so incredibly learned as to be completely incomprehensible and merely full of signs, abbreviations, and dog Latin, which I am unable even to read. As for *The Latin names of Common Plants,* it's a scholarly book on the origin of names, pleasant enough in its way, but not helpful to my purpose.

The English Flower Garden looks a bit shorter and less prosy and pedantic than the Dictionary. Let's try that first. The aconitum or monkshood, I read, is a tall and handsome herbaceous plant of the buttercup order, dangerous from its poisonous roots. "There are many names, not so many species, the best are of some value for our gardens." And then it becomes, in the circumstances, unconsciously a trifle amusing. "Few would risk their being planted where the roots could be by any chance dug up by mistake for edible roots, as they are so deadly; but almost all the kinds may be easily naturalized in copses or shrubberies away from the garden proper." So if we have got any growing at Brynmawr—and it really seems quite possible from what they say—they would be well away from the walled garden where the fruit and vegetables grow, and probably under trees. I must bear that in mind. The book continues, "They are tall plants from three to five feet high, flowering from July to September." Well, slowly we're building up a picture. Pansies, for instance, are not "three to five feet high."

As a matter of fact there is also a picture, so called, in this work, but it's a very poor thing. The Aconite appears to be a lanky plant running to seed and looking very dull. I'm

sure I should pull it up as a weed if one of those dreadful
moments arrived when my aunt compelled me to weed. She
does sometimes; but though I will keep the illustration open
beside me in case it gives me an idea, it is much too blurred
and small to be of any help at all really.

And now for the *Illustrated Dictionary*. Aconitum is named
after a harbour of Heraclea in Bithynia, near which it is said
to abound. Well, I'm not going there to get some, even if I
knew where Heraclea was and even if the author were sure,
which he doesn't seem to be. Aconite, monkshood, or wolfsbane is a very ornamental hardy perennial. I can only say
it didn't look it in the last illustration. "Flowers in terminal
racemes; sepals five, the upper one helmet-shaped, the two
sides broader than the two back ones; petals five, small, the
two upper with long claws hooded at the tip; the three inferior smaller or undeveloped; leaves palmate. Will produce
fine panicles of handsome flowers. Although very unlike
horseradish, they have frequently been mistaken for it, with
fatal results; and none of the species should be cultivated in
or near the kitchen garden." All right, all right, we all know
that by now.

Now I must admit that this man, though over technical, is
a trier, and incidentally I apologize for destroying his gram-
mar by abbreviating. If only I knew what "racemes," "sepals,"
"palmate," and "panicles" were, I should be getting on. I
suppose I must look them up in the dictionary.

However, there are also three illustrations. He appears,
however, to disagree with the man who said there were many
names, but not so many species. He lists dozens and dozens
of species, but unfortunately does not illustrate "ferox," who
appears to be the little darling for my purpose.

But, by George, this third illustration does seem familiar.
Let me think. Let me imagine that as three to five feet high,
blue or yellow—rather pale yellow seems right somehow—
growing under a tree. Yes, yes, hurrah yes, under the copper-
beech on the right of the lawn as you look out of the drawing-
room window. Undoubtedly, that's it. In full flower now, for

things are generally late at Brynmawr, and not so far from the kitchen-garden, either; though it's true there is a wall in between, there has my aunt planted and carefully tended the aconite, the old wolf shall have her bane.

This is too easy. "Kuza-uza," as the Japanese say.

5

I did not linger much longer in London after I had made up my mind. The only real thing to stay for was the dentist and he, mercifully, was not so tedious as he might have been. For the rest, it was a dead season in London—one should have been abroad—and I began to realize what a country cousin I must appear to be to all my acquaintances, by going there at such a time.

The run down to Brynmawr went off excellently. For once I was lucky with the traffic in town and, even more unusual, there were no careless pedestrians in my path. I think I should have beaten my own record from the Club to the garage by at least five minutes, if I had not been stopped just outside the gate by old Spencer. I tried hard to get past him, intending just to wave a hand and go on, but he clumsily, or perhaps intentionally, blocked the road with his muddy, untidy-looking car. I had to pull up. It would have been quite useless to attempt to explain to him why I wanted to go straight on. He has an intense loathing of other people going fast, though he goes most dangerously himself on occasion; witness his dash to my aunt when she threw herself down the side of the dingle into the blackberry bushes; nor can he understand the desire to improve on a personal performance. The triumphant thing for him is always of an athletic nature and involves beating someone else. However, here he was, hearty and bluff as usual, with his inevitable foul pipe drawing as noisily as ever, but looking rather solemn for once.

"Piece of luck, this, Edward. Spotted your car coming along. I want to talk to you before you see your aunt."

"Oh, yes!" As he leant over the edge of La Joyeuse I looked up at him from my low driving-seat and tried to dodge the clouds of tobacco smoke.

"Your aunt, Edward, is in a curiously nervous state. To be quite candid, she seems to be worrying over something I don't understand. Of course her car accident shook her nerves —shook them very badly—much worse than anybody realized at the time. The whole business, and your whole attitude at the time, Edward, seems to be weighing on her frightfully, and just now she's an absolute bundle of nerves."

"My dear doctor," I broke in, "with all due respect, what nonsense! I never knew anyone so calm and collected, and so absolutely and invariably free from nerves as my aunt."

"Normally, yes, but if you had any medical knowledge, Edward, or even any powers of observation, you would see that just now Miss Powell is emphatically not herself. I don't talk nonsense, Edward, and you know it quite well, even though respect for your elders was a thing you never had."

I shrugged my shoulders and left it at that. "Well, I'll look, but why you should put it down to me, I can't imagine. If you must know, my aunt has been rather difficult just recently, to me especially. In fact, what you call nerves I believe is just bad temper because she can't have her own way always. It's a trick a lot of old people fall into, don't you think?"

That, at any rate, was one back on old Spencer for his patronizing tone. I cannot imagine why people should be treated with respect simply because they are old. They should be treated with respect if they are worthy of respect. However, Spencer's voice was booming again in my ear.

"I can't think how you can talk in that way about your aunt, but since I believe you've really got some good in you, Edward—"

"Thank you so much," I managed to interpolate.

"—I'm going to ask you two things. Remember, Edward, all your aunt has done for you, and just think whether it isn't really up to you to relieve her of the financial worry of keeping you, and the mental worry of looking after you, by going and earning your living somehow. I must admit I don't quite know how you could, but surely you've got enough brains to do something, instead of idling your time away here. Oh, I don't mean to be harsh; it's not your fault. Your aunt ought to have put it to you long ago, but she never would do it, though I know she's been advised to often enough." (I could guess who did the advising—interfering old brute.) "But now it has been put to you, won't you think it over carefully?"

Of course I had no intention of considering doing any such thing. The mental worry of keeping me, indeed! Still, I had been thinking pretty fast while the old fellow had been spouting away so dramatically. It would be a very bad moment to arouse the suspicions of anyone, most of all, my aunt's doctor, as to my feelings for her. A soft answer now might be just the very thing to keep all *arrières pensées* away from me. For a second I kept silent as if thinking very carefully, and then answered very slowly, apparently as if weighing my words, but really to make sure that they sank in.

"Yes, certainly I will. In fact, you know I have often thought of it. Idling away my time here, as you call it, is sometimes a bit dull. I've often thought I'd like to live elsewhere, but of course Aunt Mildred is so deeply devoted to the place that one couldn't suggest moving." This was dangerous ground. The very idea, I could see, was almost sacrilege to Spencer. "But there are difficulties, you know. One can't get any job that's worth having without training, and I'm not, you know, trained to anything particular. Except, perhaps, for some form of literary career; and supposing I was to try and train for something, and I must admit I can't think of anything that attracts me, I should have to have rather a larger allowance while I was away doing it."

"That might be arranged, I believe, if your aunt was convinced that you were seriously trying to go in for whatever it was."

Of course that gave the show away. This was an embassy from my aunt, the object being to try and get rid of me at the price of a pultry allowance, and bury me in some ghastly office for life. Not for me, thank you, on any terms! Still, having seen through my aunt and Spencer's little conspiracy, there was no need to give myself away at once. It would be very easy to gain the few days' time I wanted!

"I see." (A pause.) "And what profession or occupation had you in mind?"

"Oh, this isn't a detailed plan, my dear Edward, plotted out with great care." (I could believe that or not, as I liked, but I wished he wouldn't keep on "my dear Edward"-ing me.) "For one thing she would naturally like you to choose something to which you feel you have some inclination."

I couldn't help smiling at the old boy. The idea of my solemnly expressing a preference as to which compartment of hell I preferred was too comic. I wonder what he would have said if I had expressed a desire to join the Church? He would probably have collapsed completely, and yet I am quite as suitable for a parson as I am for a lawyer, or an accountant, or a banker.

"Well, I'll think it over carefully, I promise you." The engine of La Joyeuse began to purr gently, and even Spencer took the hint.

"Good boy, Edward. I knew you'd see it if it was put to you properly; it's only a thought, but you know you have a good knowledge of the engines of cars, and that means a good mechanical brain. However, just as you like. I don't want you to feel that the choice is anything but yours. And for the next few days, while you're thinking it over, be very nice to your aunt, won't you? That's the second thing I wanted to ask you. She really does seem to be very worried. Good lad," and with that the old boy went away, positively grinning.

And well he might if he thought that his despicable plot with my aunt was likely to come off. It really is a fortunate thing that I have prepared counter-measures in advance, because otherwise, so great is my aunt's determination of character, I'm not at all certain she wouldn't force me into something of the sort. I can even see myself clad in dirty, coarse blue overalls, getting covered with oil, and apprenticed to some ghastly firm of engineers, making very indifferent lorries or something quite unsuited to the essential poetry of my nature, probably in Birmingham, which, with the possible exception of Wolverhampton, is, I understand, the very nastiest place in the world, sordid and commercial to an unparalleled degree. How can even my aunt or old Spencer possibly imagine me, in all seriousness, doing a job of work clad in blue dungarees? Or arriving at some grim factory at five in the morning, or whenever they start? Or keeping office hours? or saying, "Yes, sir," and "No, sir," to some silly consequential foreman? It would be absolutely laughable but for the fact that my aunt has a way of making her most preposterous dreams come true. She just takes things for granted and somehow or other they are so.

6

I must admit reluctantly that Spencer is right over one thing; my aunt certainly is in a nervous, fussy state. She keeps on looking at me as if she were going to say something, and then stopping, and several times I have noticed her studying me when she thought I was not looking. During meals, too, she is incessantly fumbling with a napkin-ring or a fork in a manner which is absolutely infuriating, and which I know would have called forth a sharp rebuke from her if I had done it when I was young.

Of course, having reached what must have been a major decision for her, I can quite understand that she would be very anxious to know whether I am going to fall into her little plot, and to some extent that would account for her manner, but all the same it doesn't seem enough to account for it wholly. I can never forget that she has half threatened to take action and that I don't know—one never does with my aunt—what that action is. Possibly this scheme to get rid

of me is the action, but I am not certain. I can't help thinking
that she has got something else up her sleeve, something
unpleasant which she is frightened, and even rather reluctant,
to carry out, but which she is gradually coming to the conclusion she will do if necessary. Now my aunt is a very determined woman who will not stick at trifles, and I am therefore quite sure that whatever it is she is contemplating, it is
something very drastic indeed. In fact I must admit that I
am just a little alarmed—really, to be honest, more than a
little alarmed. If I also had not made my plans, I doubt if
I should have the courage to stay in the house, or at any rate
I should simply have to clear up the situation and find out
what is in her mind. And if by any chance my plans mis-
carried and she were to find out, I should get out of the
house as fast as ever I could drive La Joyeuse. When the
day comes, and it will be either next Sunday or the Sunday
after (I shall know when I see Evans bringing up horseradish
on the Saturday evening and I shall be on the lookout for
him), I shall have everything ready for instant flight. Of
course it is very improbable that I shall need to do anything
except stay, but it will be well to have the car prepared and
a few clothes ready so that I may go. What will happen
afterwards I don't know and, on the whole, don't like to
contemplate, but the worst will probably be a temporary
exile to Birmingham, for my aunt is too devoted to our
unimportant family, too full of pride at being a Powell of
Brynmawr—though what there is to be proud of in that I do
not know—to allow any scandal to come out. And after a
short experience of me, I think I shall be able to convince
anybody she sends me to in Birmingham that he will be
happier without me, so much happier, that even my aunt
will agree. But stay on in the same house with her I could not.

Meanwhile I am rather distressed about one thing. I am no
longer quite sure that the plants I was convinced were
aconites are really aconites. The trouble is that, owing to a
misplaced scruple, I did not cut out the illustrations from the
Club's obsolete gardening-books, and so I have to rely on my

memory; but the leaves don't look quite right. Moreover, I thought they ought to be flowering now, and they aren't. However, the book said July to September and we are well on in September now, so perhaps there is nothing in that. But I should like to be sure. Of course, at the worst, if my aunt does eat a few harmless roots of some inoffensive plant nothing will happen, and I can make certain some other time. Still, it is all very wearing, and if there is any delay, Spencer and my aunt may try to jockey me into this great Birmingham idea. By the way, I tried to pull up one of the things to see if its root was tapering or not, but I could not get it really to come up whole, and I don't dare to dig for fear of giving the show away, nor did I like to risk trying to pull up more than one plant.

At this point I put my diary away in the little safe which my aunt gave me many years ago I never leave it lying about for a minute—and went down to join my aunt in the garden. I didn't see why she shouldn't supply a little useful information, and I thought that if I was tactful I should probably get it.

"Can I give you a hand, Aunt Mildred?" I began. "I don't believe you ought to take so much exercise as you do, you know. I saw Spencer for a few minutes when I came back the other day and he really seemed quite worried about you."

My aunt looked surprised, and really, I suppose, well she might. She removed half a worm from the end of her rake, while I strove fairly successfully to hide the involuntary shudder that the wriggling of bisected worms always gives me. She picked up a hoe.

"This is very sudden, Edward. I don't think I ever remember your offering to do anything in the garden before. There's plenty to be done always. As for myself, don't you worry. I'm very well able to look after myself." She threw a handful of groundsel into a wheelbarrow and added "Fortunately" below her breath.

I don't know if she intended to startle me. It's just possible she did, for I caught her looking at me sideways afterwards,

but anyhow I pretended not to have heard and went
quietly on·

"I don't know how you know what *are* weeds even, still less
how you know what you want to thin out. What were these
things, for instance?"

"Canterbury bells, my dear boy. It really doesn't take a
genius to know a weed from a flower."

I brought her back again to the point.

"Suppose so. But I do think it's difficult to know everything
by name after it's stopped flowering. And most things in this
herbaceous border have by now."

"Easy enough, if you take any interest in it, my dear Edward; after you've nearly broken your back planting out
seedlings, you begin to know what the leaves look like. Anyhow, you know groundsel by sight, and there's plenty in this
bed, so if you were really genuine when you offered to help,
you can start by pulling all that up."

It was a grim business, but if I was to get her to talk without raising her suspicions, there was nothing else for it;
besides, I was fairly caught by my own suggestion. I do hate
being taken at my word. For the best part of an hour I
slaved away, first in one bed and then in another, while my
aunt looked up occasionally to watch me with grim satisfaction. It will take weeks of care and attention to get my
finger-nails right again. Indeed, I don't think they will be
until I next have them manicured.

At the end of the hour, I found that both my aunt and I
were resting at the same moment. She grinned at me.

"Had enough, Edward?"

"Well, I think I've looked at every leaf in the whole bed,
Aunt Mildred, but as I don't know the names of any of them
I'm as wise as before. Come," I laughed gaily, "give me a
botany lesson and tell me what they all are."

For a moment I thought my aunt was going to refuse, but
after a second's hesitation she apparently came to a decision.
Down the side of the border we strolled together, my aunt's
weatherbeaten and stained skirt, and the square-toed brogues

she keeps for gardening in, contrasting oddly with my dove-gray flannel suit and neatly pointed brown shoes, my aunt discoursing continuously on this and that flower; how this one was very hardy, how that one had given her a great deal of trouble but was most attractive in the early spring, and how the other had been given her by an old crony of hers; of triumphs over rival gardeners, and unexpected and humiliating failures (I had no idea gardening was so competitive), and all the time she told me the names carefully and I repeated them, and all the time I edged her nearer to those plants underneath the tree, though not so much underneath as from memory I thought they were, whose names I really wanted to know.

The climax came very unexpectedly. I was just about to claim knowledge of one plant—a blue thing it had been, if I remember right—when my aunt suddenly said:

"And that's an aconite, Edward."

It was so unexpected that I nearly gave myself away. "*Is* it?" I said incredulously. "I thought—"

"What did you think it was, Edward?"

"I thought it was larkspur. That just shows how ignorant I am; but isn't an aconite poisonous though?"

Thinking it over afterwards, I am not sure that that wasn't a dangerous question, but my idea was to be blandly innocent and so bring off a sort of bluff. My aunt's answer was rather interesting.

"Only the root, and nobody would be such a fool as to dig it up and start eating it. That's why I keep it well away from the kitchen garden; and Evans isn't an idiot and knows all about it, of course. I shouldn't worry, Edward. Nobody will ever eat *that* by accident."

I wonder! Also I wonder whether everyone else will be so certain when the accident does occur! However.

"It's over now, anyhow, and will soon be chucked away. I hope, I must say, you won't have any more."

"Oh, it's rather pretty. Most people have it, you know. You've seen it often."

"Yes, I think I have," I passed on as if the subject didn't really interest me much. "And what are those?" I pointed to the plants which I still half believed to be aconites.

"Those? Oh, aquilegias. Columbine is the English name."

I got up an argument on English as opposed to Latin names for flowers—a safe draw, I find, with any gardener, and there, soon after, the so-called botany lesson ended.

But I am not so sure. I have seen so many of those plants my aunt called aconites and it seems almost criminally careless to have them all over the place as they are. If I thought that she, for a moment, suspected my intended use of them, I should be quite certain that she lied to me. But it is absolutely impossible that she should do anything of the sort—suspect, I mean, not lie—she's quite capable of that! That she should be mistaken is also out of the question; she is far too expert. There is, however, this possibility. There is no question but that the aconite is dangerous, and merely on general principles my aunt is just the sort of woman who would intentionally mislead me or anyone else whom she thought she could mislead about it—by pointing out the wrong plant.

Now, if there had not been any aconites in the garden, she would simply not have mentioned them. The fact that she has called something an aconite is therefore absolute proof that somewhere, and probably somewhere pretty close to the plant she has called an aconite, the genuine thing is growing. Therefore, when the time comes, I shall examine her so-called aconite—which, after all, may be the thing itself —and the thing I think is one, and everything round about in that part of the herbaceous border, for something with a tapering root. And, if necessary, the horseradish sauce will be made of a sort of salad of mixed flower roots. And if necessary we'll go on from Sunday to Sunday till by trial and error I find the right one. It will mean I shall have to watch Evans or the larder for signs of roast beef for several Saturdays, and it will mean that my alarm clock will arouse me for digging operations very early on several Sunday mornings, but one can never make omelettes without breaking eggs. I apologize to my diary for the cliché.

7

Time is dragging past wearily. We have lamb ("So much nicer in the hot weather, don't you think, dear?" "Oh, yes, Aunt Mildred—though I shouldn't like it always"—what awful platitudes); we have pigeons presented by Spencer and they provide no food for anyone, but an opportunity for my aunt to ask why I have never taken up shooting, which is a question I have answered long ago; we have steaks and chops and roast pork, "because it's a little colder today, dear," and we have veal and ham and Irish stew and liver and bacon and ducks and chickens and gammon, and tripe and onions(which is not a fit thing to give human beings to eat) and beef braised, and beef boiled, and beef minced with poached eggs, and beef turned into excellent Derby rounds, but we never have roast beef and horseradish sauce.

And we talk. Eternal platitudes about the local hospital and the peccant wanderings of Williams' cattle, and whether we shall go to the Howells' tea-party, and if I really would like a book on gardening, and the eternal debate as to whether this summer was really wetter than the one before; but we can't talk about politics because we disagree about them so violently, my aunt being actually an admirer of that futile man Baldwin, while I naturally favor the virile Mosley; nor can we discuss books without coming almost to blows, nor even whether my aunt shall sack Mary, for she still has curious ideas about me. And all the time we are both obviously watching the other, both carefully evading the subject that is constantly in our minds, and consequently both nervy, on edge, and very distinctly snappy. Soon it will be too much for me, and I shall blurt out, "And when are we next having horseradish for lunch?" For I must confess that, to my mind by now, the beef is only the trimming to the sauce. I see running always in my mind lunatic menus beginning "Potage Somnoquube," and going on ultimately to "Bœuf Rôti aux Aconits," which is anyhow absurd, as on a menu roast beef is always roast beef.

And if I am haunted by a not too yellowish, dark-colored, tapering root, I really believe my aunt is equally haunted by a vision of me in blue dungarees getting up at five in the morning to stoke the furnace, perhaps even, for she is a super-optimist, of me as a square-jawed captain of industry standing beside some deplorable machine I have invented which will put more people out of work. At least, I have the advantage of knowing what she is thinking, and avoiding the subject of Birmingham, whereas she cannot know what is in my mind, and the accidental omission of roast beef from the bill of fare is giving me time to mature the last details of my plans. My aunt has said that there must be no more accidents, and therefore there must not be. This is to be a certainty. In fact, rather too sweeping a certainty for I must admit that the revengeful cook, the faithless Mary, and that giggling kitchen-maid, Violet, are quite likely to rush all unasked into danger, though with luck that may be avoided.

And my waiting has been crowned with success.

Perhaps I should say that at any rate tomorrow morning will bring things to a head. And at the same time my aunt has removed the last trace of compunction that I felt. I had been a little inclined to call a halt, to feel sorry for the irrelevant staff of the house, and even for my aging relative. But today she finally settled it.

To begin with, she selected my own room immediately after lunch as a suitable time and place to deliver a monologue, a lecture almost, on my alleged shortcomings. I am not going to worry to put it down at length; I prefer to try and forget it, but I am afraid I shall always see her stumpy, ungainly figure standing with feet planted firmly apart on my hearthrug, talking on and on, bitterly, cruelly, and, I must add, using phrases which are only too likely to last in my memory.

She began by at last broaching the subject of Birmingham. She "had heard from dear Doctor Spencer" of our conversation, and had been delighted to hear from him that I was considering it seriously.

"Delighted, Aunt Mildred! And will you be so glad to see the back of me?"

My aunt is at least an honest woman.

"There's no need to put it so crudely, Edward; but even you will not pretend we are absolutely congenial either of us to the other," and with that she went on, stung by my silence, or perhaps the look in my eye, to confess what I had all along known of course, that Spencer's *démarche* had been entirely with her consent.

On this a silence fell, while I, very painfully aware that my afternoon's rest was ruined, wondered only if it was necessary to give any answer at all. Such a hope was, of course, a vain illusion.

"Well, Edward, I'm waiting for an answer." My aunt's voice fell sternly on my reverie like a stone dropping into a well.

It was foolish of me, I know, but I told her the truth all too plainly. I remember using phrases about "you and your precious plots with that old fool Spencer," "trying to turn me into a useless wage-slave," "your anxiety to make me do something for which I am completely unsuited in order to be free of me and my keep," "you have got rid of my dog and now you want to get rid of me." By the end it must have been tolerably clear even to my aunt that I would not go to Birmingham. It was a little crude, I know, but she is so obstinate that nothing but the clearest and most emphatic opposition will do. Had I weakened for a moment I really believe that in a trice I should have found myself "apprenticed to a pirate," to quote her favourite "poet."

Like all people who get their own way always, when she found herself thwarted, her rage was terrific. Curiously enough she started on my last remark; my reference to So-so apparently particularly stung her—conscience trouble I sup-

pose. She thundered over this. How dared I remind her of
the death of that lap-dog? (Lap-dog indeed! My poor So and!)
She would have thought I would have tried to have forgotten
that by now. But then I was always rather like that dog myself, "a poor-spirited, yapping little cur always prepared to
bite the hand that feeds you," "a mean, greedy, fat little slug
thinking only of your own comfort and how much you can eat
—ever since you were born."

"Well, you brought me up," I managed to interject.

"Yes, but you don't often seem to remember the fact."
Good heavens, as if I could ever forget it! I should like to
give her *my* version of my childhood. But my aunt's voice
went booming on, her nose, always red and uncared for, was
by now shining like a beacon with her excitement, while her
complexion had gone past the turkeycock stage and assumed
the cold white of ungovernable fury. Indeed, she clearly was
out of control. She went back to my schooldays. She cast in
my teeth my early departure from that grim establishment,
about which she was obviously cheerfully, and without question, ready to believe the worst; she abused my friends, my
books, my tastes, my clothes, my morals (Oh, yes, we had all
the Mary business over again with some new chapters
founded on an alleged incident of the last few days); she
slated me like a fishwife for being a lazy slacker, a ne'er-do-
well, an idler, "a sponger on my bounty who hasn't even the
decency to admit that he is sponging"; she descended to
personalities even. I was fat, I was pimply, my hair was too
long, my face was too puffy, and my clothes were those "of
a namby-pamby little pansy boy." If that alone had been said,
I should have sought revenge.

But still she went on. I was scorning her kind offer (kind
indeed!), I was disrespectful to Dr. Spencer, I was ungrate-
ful, I wasn't prepared to do a hand's turn to earn an honest
penny. I was this, that, and the other. I could stand it no
longer. Really, I don't know how I stood it so long. I got up
and prepared to go.

"When you are yourself again, Aunt Mildred, we may

perhaps continue the discussion, though I think it would really be better if none of these topics were ever mentioned again. But at present I refuse to listen to any more.

I moved to the door, but my aunt was too quick for me. She leapt towards it and, with her back to it, prevented me from going out, while she continued to rate me. But this time there was a different note in her voice; clearly she was starting to regain control of herself.

"Perhaps so, Edward. I think there is no need for me to say any more. You know now what I feel. But let this be quite clear. You will behave yourself in future, Edward. You understand me, don't you? You will behave yourself; and you will start work somewhere within a month if we can find anywhere where they will take you—which may be difficult. If we can, you will go. If not, you will give me a solemn promise to go where and when I send you, or I shall take action. I know exactly, Edward, what I intend to do. More clearly than you think you do; and, let me once more repeat, in the meantime you will behave yourself, or— Now you may open the door for me."

Somewhat feebly I did, and she swept out, trying to look like Queen Elizabeth and, I need hardly say, failing abominably.

For myself, I went out into the garden to cool my head, and there I met Evans carrying in some leaves with long roots, yellowish in color, and not tapering. Through the larder window, despite the zinc sieve to keep the flies out, I could see a joint of beef hanging. My alarm clock is set for dawn, my precautions, including luggage packed, and petrol in La Joyeuse, all are taken. I wonder, by way, if Cook makes that sauce overnight? It won't matter if she does, I can grate some of the stuff in, but anyhow, one way or another the great substitution will be made tomorrow morning, and by lunch time the whole thing will be decided. Before tea time it will be all over. I shall probably have to get my own tea.

5: *Postscript*

IT was so like poor Edward that he should object to giving a hand to put the netting over the cherry trees, although he was the only person who really liked that sort of cherry. It was so like him to go to all that trouble to pretend that he had not walked that early summer afternoon into Llwll. And I suppose, to be fair, that it was extremely characteristic of me that I should take such a great deal of trouble to see that he did.

There were really several reasons. First of all, if one lives in the country one must take good care to prevent one's brains rusting, and nothing improves them so much as a little battle of wits of that sort. Then I must admit that it was most amusing. The sight of Edward sweating and panting as he struggled out of the Fron Wood was alone worth the trouble, and his efforts to appear at the time as if he had not stirred a yard except in that vulgar little car of his were absolutely ludicrous. I don't know how I kept a straight face, for, of course, I had to, since it was definitely part of the fun not to let him know too soon, not until he had exhausted his last little bit of energy on putting up the cherry-netting, that I knew all about his afternoon's performance, had telephoned before and after to Herbertson and Hughes—two such nice reliable men—had even got the telephone girl to help me, and had actually seen him come back. In fact that I had stage-managed the whole marionette show while he was only a puppet, though a puppet playing an important part. As a matter of fact there was one detail which was an accident, namely that he got those few drops of petrol, and there, I must admit, fate was good to me.

But the affair was not only a comedy got up by me to pass an idle afternoon laughing at my nephew. There was a certain objective behind it. Since his earliest days Edward has always been a difficult person to control. In his very cradle he was the most obstinate baby I have ever heard of, and as a small boy he was a holy terror. If, for one minute, his imperial will was thwarted, there were tears and exhibitions of temper, followed by fits of sullenness and a determination to obtain his way somehow. I remember that once some toy or other was taken from him temporarily—he had plenty of others at the time and this one was neglected. Instantly, of course, that was the one thing he wanted and, when he found that screams and sobs were useless, he apparently quietened down. But that night he got up in the middle of the night and smashed every single thing in the nursery that he could break of which he thought his nurse was fond.

I do not know if I am to blame for his upbringing. Goodness knows, it's hard enough to bring up a child anyhow, and especially a headstrong boy who is not your own and who had such parents. I want to say as little as possible about my poor brother, but he was, I am afraid, not a very well-balanced man, and there has always been a mystery about the tragedy of his and his wife's death. Of course, we always tried to keep any reference to it away from Edward, but apparently some inkling of it reached him. He was too young to be affected by the shock of it, but with such a parent he was almost bound to be difficult.

But it was clear that if he kept the spirit he showed in the nursery throughout his life, he would have a very poor time of it. The world will not stand someone who insists that he is always in the right, who must always have his own way, and who, when crossed, is revengeful and bears malice. So, rather reluctantly, I was forced to try to be kind, but in-

credibly firm. Whenever Edward laid down the law, about
however trivial a point, I made it an absolute rule to defeat
him. It was rather hard work at times, but I was very seldom
unsuccessful. Part of it, of course, was pure bluff, and hence
grew up the use of the phrase "I shall take action." I thought,
as I now know, that it had some sort of mesmeric influence
over him and very often it was only necessary to use it,
and the occasion of having to put the threat into force was
over.

Yet, on the whole, and though I cannot see what other
course I could have pursued, the system has not been entirely successful. Edward remained as obstinate and selfish
and difficult as ever. That I knew, but I had not entirely
realized that he still treasured up ill will to such an extent.
On looking back at it, I cannot help giving him a sort of
grudging admiration. Not everyone would have stood the
training he got and remained entirely unaltered, especially
such an essentially futile person as Edward, a youth so very
effeminate in appearance and tastes. Yes, undoubtedly Edward had character, even if it was rather an unpleasant character, but it did make his life rather an unhappy one.

His nursery was one long battle, his schooldays nothing
but a fiasco, a whole series of them. We tried school after
school, and he came back from each of them in a white heat
of fury and went to the next with a determination to be
miserable. There never was anyone the equal of Edward at
cutting off his nose to spite his face; and if the various
schools were not approved of by Edward, they returned the
compliment. Some asked me to take him away outright; all
heaved a sigh of relief when he went, and finally there was
a very unpleasant scandal to which I will not refer except
briefly. In a fury of rage he defaced some relics of great
sentimental value to the school, and was almost lynched. Yes,
certainly his schooldays were unhappy, but on the whole I
have come to the conclusion that the boys who complain that
they had a miserable time at private or public schools have
usually thoroughly deserved it.

However, after that, I gave up the effort of sending him to school any longer. Indeed, I think no school would have taken him. There remained the problem of what to do with his life. Since I had failed in the matter of his education, I rather feebly allowed things to drift, hoping always that he would strike out some line for himself—a vain hope, as I now see, but the only one I could think of. Meanwhile, I provided a home and a very reasonable allowance for him, ample for his needs while he lived with me, which he had the grace to acknowledge, but not enough to let him be entirely independent with his tastes unless he took his coat off and worked. Besides, it was all I could really afford.

Of course I might have forced him by financial pressure to do something, and I think that ultimately I might have had recourse to that, but I am sure that under pressure Edward would have deliberately failed at anything he was forced to do. Besides, I had promised his parents, and that promise I held sacred. Also he was the last of the Powells of Brynmawr and I did desperately hope he would take to our dear old house and the lovely country round it. A vain hope, I fear.

Knowing Edward as I did, I ought to have known that such an incident as his walk to Llwll would rankle. But, you know, Edward looked so insignificant, so futile, and was, in fact, so incompetent, that, after defeating him for so many years, I had rather got into the habit of underrating him; and, as to that trivial business, I had forgotten one thing. I had forgotten that I had laughed at him openly, a thing no one likes, and Edward never could stand, and which I generally managed to avoid; and so from that little comedy the whole thing started, and as, perhaps, I was responsible (well, possibly there is "perhaps" about it) for the start, I suppose I am in a way responsible for the finish, so I have edited Edward's diary so that the dates and the names are a little confused, for there are reasons why I should not like the identity of myself and Brynmawr too clearly revealed, as you will see at the end, and now in fairness I propose to write the postscript that is necessary as an explanation.

2

Really the credit for the fact that I am still alive must go mainly to dear Dr. Spencer. I say "mainly," not "entirely," only because it was pure good luck that I was not killed straight away when Edward cut through the brakes of my car. That was a very well-engineered accident; indeed, Edward always did have an excellent mechanical knowledge, which I always wanted him to put to some useful purpose, but in other respects it was not so clever. You see, Edward fondly thought he had left no traces of any kind, and in point of fact there were a great many.

To begin with, as he himself knew, it was essential there should be no suspicion, simply because he was certain to be a bad witness. But, in fact, he attracted attention to himself straight away by the oddness of his manner at the time. His whole appearance was funny, so funny that Dr. Spencer, who is a singularly shrewd man beneath a benign appearance, thought it peculiar even when his attention was almost wholly occupied in looking after me. Edward was so anxious on the one hand to speak of his great anxiety, and on the other to do absolutely nothing to help, his face was so very white and strained, his movements so jerky, and his conviction that I was dead so very fixed, that, in all, it seemed curious.

Accordingly, after he had made me as comfortable as he could, the Doctor began to make a few inquiries. To begin with, he rather wanted to know what had happened and how it had happened, and whether anyone had seen it. On the way down from my bedroom he found my beloved old Cook, the most loyal person in the world, in a terrible state of grief, and set to work to calm her nerves.

"Now, Cook," he said, "we must all do what we can to help Miss Powell, and so we must all keep our heads and be calm and helpful. I think she'll pull through probably" (and I understand at that the dear old thing positively sobbed), "so

I want you to be quite cheerful and normal. Now just help me a bit. Did any of you see the accident?"

"Oh, no, sir, I was in the kitchen, and the first thing I heard was a crash; at least, I thought I did, and I went to the front hall and I couldn't see anything, so after a bit I went back to the kitchen, but I couldn't settle down to anything somehow. You know, sir, how you do get a feeling when anything's wrong, don't you? and then some minutes later I heard Master Edward come in and go to the telephone, and I'm afraid I listened, sir."

The doctor smiled gently at that. As a matter of fact it was fairly well known that Cook generally did listen!

"Well, never mind that, Cook. But do you happen to know if Mr. Edward saw anything?"

"I really couldn't say, sir, but he might, because his little dog seems to have been the cause of the disaster, sir (the little dog's killed, sir), and Master Edward said then that her car was at the bottom of the dingle, but he thought she'd been thrown out, and so she had been, poor lady."

"It's as well she was, Cook, she'd have had a poor chance in the car. I suppose the crash you heard was only just before Mr. Edward came back?"

"Oh, no, sir, at least five minutes before, possibly ten."

"I see. Then Mr. Edward must have investigated a bit before he telephoned to me. Stupid of him. He ought to have got me at once."

Cook looked at him rather hard at that. "It's my belief," she snapped, "that he was more concerned about that dog. He'd wrapped him up carefully in a duster and put him on a table, and a shocking mess it'll be in too."

Dr. Spencer closed the conversation and gave her something to do by commiserating with her on the work she would have in cleaning up. He had suddenly remembered that Edward had shown most emotion when he had said I was *not* dead! His agonized "Oh, my God!" had sounded really genuine then. Just as he reached the foot of the stairs, Cook called him back.

"But I never really answered your question just now, sir, about seeing the accident. I've just been giving Master Edward a nice cup of tea, him being so upset, and I said to him, 'and you seeing it and all,' and he said, 'No, not quite, Cook,' but I don't quite know what he meant by that."

With that in his mind Dr. Spencer went down to talk to Edward, and that conversation has been reasonably faithfully recorded in Edward's diary. But there were several points which emerged from it which Edward certainly did not realize, although, to do him justice, he did think of some of them. Dr. Spencer, a most methodical man, gave me afterwards the notes he put down at the time for investigation later.

1. E. told Cook he didn't quite see the accident. He told me he saw the car going over the edge and then it went out of sight. Note. Look at spot and see if from inside meadow you could see car go over edge and if it would go out of sight.

2. E. says he saw car crash into bottom of dingle. Note. Can you see and how quickly could he get across fence. Any signs of break through?

3. E. thought he saw aunt in bush. What would he have seen?

4. What was E. doing in that field? Not his shortest way home. There never were any mushrooms in it.

5. Look at apple and damson crop.

6. Why this long pause?

You will see that within an hour or two Dr. Spencer had put his finger on several weak points in the story, and this was the man whom Edward presumed to consider a fool!

Well, naturally Dr. Spencer didn't leave it at that. He tells me he made a thorough examination of the ground straight away. So far as the apples and damsons were concerned, Edward was quite right. So he certainly had been past the orchard recently, and, moreover, past it, not in it, because while there were no damsons on the trees you could see from the meadow there were some on a tree right inside the orchard, which was not visible from the outside. But there was absolutely nothing that Dr. Spencer could see which Edward could possibly, for a second, have mistaken for a mushroom. However, a piece of paper might have blown away, or there might have been the sun glistening on a leaf then, whereas by the time the doctor had finished the shadow of Yr Allt was beginning to creep across the grass.

Now, as to what he would have seen, Edward had been pretty careful. Standing by the fence he could see the car start to go over, and then it would disappear. But in that case, why hadn't I seen him? And subsequently when Dr. Spencer asked me, I had no recollection of seeing Edward. I thought it over afterwards with great care, and I was almost certain I hadn't. Of course the concussion might have made me forget, and at the time we put it down to that, but we were never quite happy about the point, and, as we now know, we were on the right track, for I should have seen Edward if he hadn't been crouching down.

The next point was how he got over the fence quickly enough to see the car crash at the bottom of the dingle. This had quite an easy explanation, Dr. Spencer found. There was a convenient bit of timber, put in clearly to mend the fence and stop Williams' cattle from straying, which in course of time had slipped over sideways and made almost a stile. The only thing was, it was almost too convenient!

There was still the long pause to account for. The crash Cook heard must have been when the car either hit a tree or reached the bottom, probably the latter, but in any case, within a few seconds of it Edward would, by his own account, have been standing in the road. It would not have taken him two minutes to have reached the telephone. Even allowing for examining and picking up his Pekingese, well under four would be ample, and really fond though he was of the dog, he oughtn't to have spent long looking after him when he knew his aunt was at least hurt, and every minute might be vital. Yet it was five or ten minutes before he actually telephoned, according to Cook. It seemed curious to

Dr. Spencer. He may have seemed "an inquisitive old fool" to Edward, but they were pretty pertinent questions.

The next thing he did was to check up about the time. It was all very well for Cook to say, "at least five, possibly ten minutes," but she might be wrong, but curiously enough it was possible to check it up much more accurately than that.

In the first place, Edward had commented on the speed at which my old friend had arrived (By the way, what a dangerous drive that must have been!), and that had fixed in his mind the fact that he had been rung up by Edward at five minutes past four. At least, that was the time he had put down the receiver. Say three or four minutes past when Edward had rung up. Now he imagined, when he was talking to Edward, that the accident was only three or four minutes before—that, at least, was the impression Edward was giving —and that was why he made the comment that I should have been late for my hospital meeting at four o'clock. Only a minute or two late, and there would have been nothing remarkable in that if I had not been rather notoriously a punctual person. In fact, I believe I am rather a nuisance about it.

Of course Edward gave a very rational explanation of it. I had had a rush owing to the pea-sticks (and the absence of Edward to help me—an absence which generally occurred when there was a job of work to be done), but when Dr. Spencer suggested to me that I was going to be late, I was so indignant that he maintains my temperature went up and I nearly had a relapse!

As a result of that he went down to see Herbertson. Now Herbertson is a very typical Welshman. Not only in his appearance and manner (and he is, in fact, the typical dark, reserved, shortish kind of man with his knees slightly bent from a youth spent walking up hills) but in his character; once convince him that you are friendly to him and always going to act straight by him, and he will take an infinity of trouble for you; but get the wrong side of him once and you're on the wrong side for ever. And Edward was definitely and always (and on the whole deservedly) on the wrong side. No one had enjoyed the little comedy of the petrol more than Herbertson.

But there was no doubt that when Dr. Spencer asked to see the remains of my car, which, with great difficulty, Herbertson had extracted from the dingle and taken to his garage, there was a great deal of relief on his face.

"Yes, indeed, sir, I shall be glad, only too glad to show you what remains of Miss Powell's car. I would like you, sir, to examine it all yourself most carefully before I am saying anything to you."

"By all means, Herbertson. But why? You aren't suggesting I'm going to tell you something about cars you don't know? As a matter of fact I only want to look at the clock."

"The clock?" Herbertson bent over the battered and twisted bits of metal. "I expect she is in pieces. Were you thinking she would go again? She has stopped, you see, at seven minutes to four o'clock, and I think she will never reach the hour by the look of her; but do you take her, sir, and show her to Miss Powell."

"As a matter of fact, Herbertson, you've told me what I wanted to know; but what do you want me to look at?"

Herbertson scratched his head. "Look," he said, "I have, it seems, told you what you wanted without knowing what you wanted. Will you not do the same for me?"

Dr. Spencer laughed good-humouredly. "All right, Herbertson. But I did say 'Look at the clock.' What part of this mess am I to look at?"

Herbertson became grave. "The brakes, sir, the brakes."

Some few minutes later, Dr. Spencer looked up equally seriously. "You're right, Herbertson. No stones, or anything like that, could have caused cuts so new and so clean."

"No. And look you, we can guess here. I may be only the manager of the Wynneland Garage who isn't good enough to sell some little beasts petrol, but I have got eyes, and I am not quite without brains."

"Yes, and please, Herbertson, with also the sense to keep

your mouth shut. This isn't proved, but if you're right in your guess—and you know it's only an absolute guess with no evidence behind it—it's for Miss Powell to decide what to do."

And here Herbertson showed what a genuine man he was. He believed, I subsequently found out, that he was making himself liable as an accomplice after the fact and might end by going to prison for it; but he was quite prepared to leave the whole thing to Dr. Spencer and me, simply because he trusted us implicitly.

3

After that my old friend felt that he ought to take me into his confidence, especially as he now considered that I was sufficiently recovered from the shock of the accident to stand this new strain.

Naturally, at first I refused to believe it. I don't think I had ever been under any very great illusions as to the extent of Edward's affection for me, but it was one thing to believe that he showed no gratitude and little affection, another to believe that he was prepared to murder me. Looking back on it I can see that perhaps I had, in a way, always kept too tight a curb on him; yet in another the curb had not been tight enough, since it had not been effective.

Gradually, however, Dr. Spencer persuaded me to examine the evidence, and, on the whole, pretty flimsy I thought it at first. There were really only two main points, the delay and the breaks. Now, as to the first of those, I felt there might easily be some simple, natural explanation. As a matter of fact, I now know there was. Really, it was hard lines on Edward that his one and only decent natural feeling, the revulsion that made him physically sick, should have been one of the first causes of our suspecting him, but there it was. Things aren't always quite fair.

Then as to the brakes, it was all very well for Dr. Spencer and Herbertson to be so confident, but it seemed to me that they were jumping to conclusions and assuming what was only suspicion to be fact. After all, mightn't something have started a cut in the brake cables and the final accident have made them snap so that the break would look like a clean cut? For instance, running through Abercwm is a canal which passes under the main road to the south, very frequently beneath a series of sharply humpbacked bridges, and these bridges are well known as a local peculiarity. Any car driver round here knows how careful you have to be over them because their steepness makes them practically blind. I have often noticed that cars with a low clearance practically touch the ground as they cross their arched tops. Well, then, mightn't I have scraped the brakes against them? I only throw it out as a suggestion indicative of what was in my mind. I don't want to lay down the law about it, because, unlike Edward, I'm no great mechanic and not quite sure offhand where the brakes are. All the same, as the sequel will show, I'm not quite ignorant of the geography of cars.

But getting back from this red herring, I didn't really feel certain about it, and nothing Dr. Spencer could say about the minor points of the case would convince me. I think, really, that though in my heart I was gradually beginning to see that the doctor was right, it was simply a case of refusing to believe what I did not want to believe. And then there came a further little bit of evidence.

I had made up my mind that the point where I had driven straight off the road was perhaps rather a dangerous one, and so I had some slight alterations made, a small bank which would, for all practical purposes, prevent any repetition of such a thing. One morning I was just seeing how the work was getting on, for though I am deeply fond of everyone in Llwll (which, by the way, is very beautiful and quite easy to pronounce), I know that, as workmen, they need constant supervision—well, while I was doing this, Llewellyn Williams came up to me and said he wanted to talk to me.

It was a little ruefully that I walked a few yards down the road with him. I know what talks with him generally mean,

and really I think I have helped him out of troubles very
nearly enough times. But this time it was not another baby,
nor a fine for being drunk on market-day, not a new roof for
his pigsty, not even a loan for just a few days. It was Edward.

Edward apparently had been breaking down his fence
again. He led me to the piece of timber which, as Dr. Spencer
had already pointed out to me, had made so convenient a
stile for Edward to hurry over and see me and my car de-
scending.

"But, Mr. Williams, I don't understand. I can see that someone could get over the fence here easily—in fact it rather
looks as if someone had—but the fence is perfectly good and
sound."

"Yes, indeed, Miss Powell, but look you, that is not the
trouble. Here the fence is good, yes, but it is not good where
this stake has been taken from. I would not like to trouble
you, Miss Powell, but on the other side of the field where this
was, there is now a gap once more open which I had closed
with it."

"How can you know it's the same stake, Mr. Williams?"

"Look you, there was a gap. I filled it. Now there is once
more a gap and no sign of the timber I put in. Here is the
same, or, at least, very much the same timber, and tell me
now why should there be any stake here? You see, there is
no need. The fence is sound without." And, indeed, when he
pulled away the offending piece he left behind a perfectly
good fence.

"I'm sorry about the gap, Mr. Williams. If there's any
reason for thinking it's anything to do with Mr. Edward, I'll
have it filled up." Privately I could not help thinking this
was just another of Williams' devices for getting me to do
what was really his job. I half expected to find some colossal
yawning cavern which could never have been filled by so
little wood as had been removed from the fence. Williams'
next words, however, showed that that was certainly the
wrong tack.

"As for the gap, Miss Powell, I would not be worrying you, she will be easily mended. But I would prove to you that you might not think I was talking at random, look you, that I have some reason for thinking this was Mr. Edward."

"And that was?"

And thereupon Williams described to me how he had encountered Edward's Pekingese scurrying across the road away from an invisible but present Edward at this very spot, and how the dog had amazingly found a biscuit on the other side of the road, and of the attempts he had made to make friends with So-so and indirectly with Edward, and of his failure to make any progress with either of them. If it had ended there it would have been strange enough, but Williams went on to explain that he had seen Edward and his dog there on at least one other occasion, and he thought on two others, though he was not sure. Clearly, then, this was at least a regular spot where So-so was taught a trick, and that was why he had bolted across the road so recklessly in front of me. That, too, accounted for Edward's concern about our special crinkly biscuits. Poor Edward! and I had thought it was all greed!

However, the immediate thing was to stop Williams from talking—a bit of a problem, for Williams is not exactly a silent gentleman at any time, and as for market-day— And how to put it I did not know, for clearly Williams had his suspicions and I did not want to seem to agree with him. At the same time, if I seemed too blind he might go on brooding over it, and then he might go talking to goodness knows whom and the fat might be properly in the fire. Fortunately he talked so long, and repeated himself so much, that I was able to think out a plan.

"Look, Mr. Williams, I think I can guess what's in your mind; and, in fact, since you've told me this I see the whole thing. Poor Mr. Edward has been hinting to me that a new trick he was teaching So-so was responsible for my accident. Of course it wasn't really, it was the brakes of the car, and that" (I managed to giggle) "was nothing to do with So-so.

But Mr. Edward has been most frightfully worried about it, and I've only just managed to reassure him, so I want the whole thing forgotten now. Besides, Dr. Spencer says it's better for my health that no more should be said about it. So, just as a favor, Mr. Williams, thank you very much for telling me, very much indeed, but would you, now I know, forget it and not talk to anyone about it?"

It was obviously difficult for Williams to do it, and eventually I had to agree that he might talk to Dr. Spencer about it if he wanted to. Clearly Williams felt I had to be more on my guard and found the "accident" a bit hard to swallow; but finally I got him to agree that I knew best, or at any rate that Dr. Spencer and I together knew best, and he went off perplexed and I think not quite sure that he had done his duty, but, on the whole, reluctantly convinced. I felt I could rely on him unless anything unforeseen stirred him up. But I had to suppress firmly Edward's ghastly tombstone for So-so. If Williams had heard of it he'd have blown up. And for that matter So-so, a dog with a certain amount of taste and, I really believe, a sense of humor—at least no Pekingese will consent to be made a fool of—would certainly have turned in his grave and probably haunted the place till we had it removed.

But, after that, even I found it harder to keep up my belief in Edward's entire innocence.

Naturally I told Dr. Spencer all about it, and unfortunately some chance words came to the ears of Mrs. Spencer and Jack. On the whole it was a relief to let these old friends into my confidence; I don't know why telling someone else about one's troubles helps, but it does. We were discussing it on the night they all came to dinner, before Edward, late as usual, came down. I must admit that his arrival caused a certain restraint, and Violet Spencer is no actress! I'm not surprised that even Edward noticed her frantic and terrified expression when he began to ask at dinner how you set fire to things.

I must own that I was a little slower than the rest of them in realizing the object in Edward's remarks. Once more poor Edward thought he was being so clever, and once more he gave himself away hopelessly. Violet, I think, spotted it first, but all three of them got there in a very short time, and then everyone had to do some very quick thinking as to how to act. Violet, as I say, knowing she was no actress, simply retired into her shell and looked so miserable that she nearly gave the show away. Jack, who had to answer, at first passed the thing off quite neatly; in fact, if nobody had wanted him to, Edward would never have got his information as to how to light his little bonfire.

But then, to the amazement of Violet, Jack, and myself, Dr. Spencer suddenly gave him a hand. I could hardly believe my ears when he suddenly chipped in, revived the flagging conversation, and threw an obvious cue to Jack to give Edward the information he wanted.

"But why did you do it?" I asked him afterwards. "If you're afraid of Edward having some design which involves this fire, why tell him how to do it?"

"Because, my dear lady, forewarned is forearmed. Because if we know what Edward's plans are, that is, assuming he has any, and I hope he hasn't, we can defeat them. Because, if you won't do what I once more implore you to do and tackle Edward direct, or let me tackle him for you, we must use our brains to keep one move in front of him. That's why I threw that cue bid, slam invitation as the contract players would say, to Jack. Don't you think he picked it up neatly?"

"I do, but where are we? We know now that somewhere, some time, Edward intends to burn something. What? When?"

"When's clear enough. Obviously if he wants a delayed fire it's to give himself time to get away. Therefore 'when' is the next time or the next time but one that he spends a week-end, or even a night, elsewhere. Edward's not very subtle, and if we watch him we shall see his preparations, I haven't the least doubt. But as to what he wants to burn, I'm afraid we know that too. Oh, don't start to deny it—"

"But I will. I can't believe it of him."

"You're incorrigible. Once more, do let me tackle him; I don't like all the suspense and worry there is for you. Let alone the danger, and, even if we do keep our wits about us, there is danger. Now, mayn't I?"

"No. If anyone talks to him, I do. And I'm going to see if I can't control him without that. After all, life here is going to be pretty odd after that talk whether he admits it or not, isn't it? Besides, while Edward doesn't realize how much we know he'll go on giving himself away as he did last night. Let him know we're suspicious and he'll be more careful. Let me try my own way for a bit longer."

"You're a brave woman; but," Dr. Spencer smiled sadly, "I think you're a foolish one, you know."

I suppose he was right, really; but I had made up my mind to watch Edward carefully and see if our suspicions were proved. If they were wrong, no one would be more glad than I. If they were right, I would make his second plan fail completely, drop a threat of "taking action"—at that time I had not made the decision I subsequently made as to what that action was to be—and hope that would frighten him off the idea altogether. Perhaps the shock of a second failure would sober him down completely, and that was what I passionately wanted. I wanted no scandal to come near the Powells of Brynmawr—his father had done all too much in that way already—and I wanted Edward to settle down and carry on the family traditions—even, as Edward would have said, to the extent of keeping the window-sills painted anchovy pink. Such a nice color really.

The next incident was positively comic.

So far as I could make out at the time, Edward came down to dinner looking portentously solemn—his face always gives him away, and I always knew when he was concealing anything—drank no more than usual at dinner so far as I could see, but by the end was apparently so intoxicated that he very nearly slipped under the table. When he went off to bed almost immediately after he started his coffee, yawning prodigiously and nodding helplessly in his chair, I thought he had had the good sense to tumble to the fact that his conversation for the last half-hour had been utterly and ludicrously incoherent, and had decided to sleep it off.

But I couldn't think how on earth the boy had got so drunk. It certainly wasn't during dinner, so I presumed he had taken to drink secretly before dinner. A fine old time I had trying to rack my brains as to what had disappeared out of what decanters during the previous day. Finally I came to the conclusion that nothing very much had, so I was forced to think that he must have some store of his own, and that was a thing I was not going to allow.

Accordingly I hunted round, and the first thing I found was a bottle of absinth, and naturally I thought I had got to the bottom of the trouble. I confiscated the bottle, of course, and I must say I was surprised that Edward made no fuss about it. Really, to this day, I don't know why. I suppose he was a little ashamed of it, and that, coupled with the fact that he didn't really like it, made him say nothing. But at the time I merely took it to mean that he had some more somewhere else, and so I redoubled my search.

I am aware that it is not a very ladylike thing to search someone else's possessions thoroughly for concealed bottles of spirits, and I blush a little to write it, but really I think it was excusable. It was a fixed idea of mine that Edward had to be controlled and, with the example of Edward's grandfather known to me, excessive drinking had to be stopped. But I went on to do a far less ladylike thing. I did, in fact, possess a key of Edward's safe. I examined the safe and found therein Edward's diary, and not only did I read it then and there, but from that time onwards I continued to read it regularly. Of course, the first thing I found out was that Edward's trouble was not absinth, but a Somnoquube. What a word! After a time I really began almost to look forward to reading it, to seeing what new and amazing perversions Edward could put on my motives. But during all the fire incident the chief effect was to give me a feeling of terrific power and security.

For now I could let Edward do what he liked. I could lead him straight up the garden path and let him down at the other end with an almighty bump.

I read with great amusement how well Edward thought he had got out of Dr. Spencer's question about the time and the clock on the car; in fact, his too ready explanation only made the doctor more suspicious, and if he did make me wince a bit occasionally in the things he said about me, I forgot it all in the fun I had watching his preparations. But let me, though I anticipate, say once and for all that I never read any of the dirty passages in Edward's French books. I wouldn't do such a thing. Edward's diary was perhaps the worst thing I ever read. For that suggestion I made up my mind he should pay, and on the whole I thought the most appropriate way that he could pay was by his own fire burning his own books.

Unfortunately, Edward thought of that too. Of course his little plan involved burning them all as an unfortunate incident in the burning of me, and my little plan was more modest. Still, he did defeat me by taking them away to be, nominally, rebound—and I am sure he took the worst. By the way, he didn't bring them all back, and I should like to know where they are, for they really oughtn't to remain undestroyed, I gather.

Of course, any fool would have smelt a rat when Edward made all those stupendous preparations to go away. By the time he'd taken his clothes to be pressed and cleaned (and insulted Mary and me in the process) and packed up a few things to dazzle the friends of the well-dressed Guy Innes, there was practically nothing left in his bedroom. Indeed, Mary began to wonder what on earth was happening.

As a matter of fact Edward was making himself much more objectionable to the unfortunate girl than you would imagine from what he says. So much so that, seeing all the packing, she got a confused idea in her head that he wanted her to run away with him for ever, which was a thing she was not going to do under any circumstances. I don't quite remember when it was she came and complained to me of Edward's behavior, but it was a very circumstantial story and I had no hesitation in believing it. That matter I did speak to Edward about, but his account leaves a good deal out.

Once, indeed, I nearly gave myself away. Edward's experiments, of course, were rather a scream, and his miscellaneous purchases in Shrewsbury distinctly amused me; but it was rather a nuisance when, instead of crawling many miles from the house and trying to work it out in a gravel pit or wherever he did go, he started to do things in Brynmawr. All the same I oughtn't to have said so bluntly that he had fused all the lights—I ought to have made out I was deceived by his very inferior pretense of finding out that the lights wouldn't work. As a matter of fact I was a little rattled by his hypocritical solicitude for my "old eyes." Old, indeed! I can see as well as any young person, and, moreover, I am not so very old.

4

However, so things went on until Edward set out for his visit to that horrible Guy Innes—really I think Edward's description is quite damning enough without further words from me—and I was left to be burnt alive; though really, as a matter of fact, I'd never thought of it that way. I was much too much enjoying the whole comedy to feel in the least worried.

As Edward disappeared down the drive I watched him and laughed heartily at the awful state I knew him to be in. I was going to have lots of fun during the ensuing night, and I felt quite safe, having just got in a new, large, and splendid supply of fire-extinguishers all unknown to Edward, but specially for his benefit.

Of course the first thing to do was to see where his infernal machine was. It wasn't very hard to find, as Edward's room was nearly empty except for the furniture. That in itself was not surprising, for it had been almost impossible to see him for the luggage piled up in his car. Really it only had the effect of making my search easier, and a very few minutes' rummaging in half-empty drawers brought me to the wardrobe. That gave me a little problem. I could find a duplicate key in all probability, but was it worth while looking for it? Supposing I found it and opened it, was I going to alter Edward's arrangements, or should I leave them? You see, I had made up my mind to have the fire, both to burn what books were left and also for realism; but if I made no alteration, it might mean that I had got to sit up half the night, because, while I did not know what time Edward had fixed on for his party, it was certain to be pretty late, so that I (and everyone else) should be soundly asleep.

Well, I don't like staying up frightfully late as a rule, but I don't mind occasionally, and I happened to have a book I wanted to read and a Women's Institute report to write, so I decided to do it. Besides, even if I did find the key, I wanted the time-machine to work—I wasn't just going to put a match to it, it mightn't have burnt the right way—and I didn't know how to alter his clock so that it went off, so to speak, at a different and earlier hour. So I just re-read the directions for using the fire-extinguishers and put the subject clean out of my mind. Really, I couldn't be bothered to let Edward occupy the whole of my existence; I'd plenty of other things to do.

As a matter of fact I nearly forgot the silly boy too completely, only fortunately I noticed that the first gulp of my coffee tasted a little odd, and remembered his beastly cubes just in time. As it was, I had a terrific struggle, even with the little I had taken, to fight sleep off. For a couple of hours I really wasn't quite sure what I was doing, the objects in the room seemed either to come towards me vastly enlarged in size, or to recede into the infinite distance. I just had sufficient sense to pour the rest of the coffee out of the window where, curiously enough, I found afterwards that several of the salpiglossis died—but that may have been a coincidence—

and to keep going until it began to pass off. By that time the maids had gone to bed and I went out and made myself some fresh and very strong coffee and went up to Edward's room.

I had plenty of time to select exactly what should be burnt, and originally I intended to make a careful choice, but unfortunately I couldn't do that. It was impossible to make a selective fire without Edward knowing I had arranged it, and I couldn't yet bring myself to an open declaration. Besides, he would want to claim from the Insurance Company, and that would mean inquiries, rather awkward inquiries possibly, apart from the question of common honesty. I felt quite bad enough about the car as it was. No, on the whole, there must be no fire claim. I must just grin and bear the loss of the wardrobe and the bookcase and the damage to the wallpaper (anyhow, Edward's room wanted repapering) and prevent any claim being made somehow. Reluctantly I returned to their drawer some particularly offensive crimson shirts and a pair of mauve and lemon pyjamas, and waited.

But I had a shockingly long time to wait. I finished my report and grew tired of reading, and still the mine hadn't gone up. Supposing Edward's mechanics were so incompetent that the thing never started? In that case I couldn't go to bed until Edward chose to return! And that might be a week! I pulled myself together and decided that if something didn't happen in half an hour I would open the wardrobe door somehow. Meanwhile, I turned spiteful and worked out my plans for the next day with the object of giving the maximum pain to Edward. On the whole, I think, after reading his account of it, that I was successful in that. It was then, too, that I decided on my final plans.

All this took time and my half-hour was long past, and my mind was far away in the future, when I realized with a start that there was crackling coming from inside the wardrobe and a little smoke coming out. It took a little nerve to let it go on. Very soon I was able to poke the flames through the side and guide the fire up to the bookcase with some firewood I had brought for the purpose, and so cause traces of fire on the wall and all over the bookcase. By that time I thought I had risked enough, and in, I must admit, a slight panic, worked my fire-extinguishers until I had got the fire completely out. As a matter of fact, I was only just in time to save a real fire, but, to my annoyance, rather too early for the efficient burning of Edward's beastly books. However, I completed that job at the remains of the kitchen fire and retired to bed very weary, but quite happy.

The next morning I took breakfast in bed—a thing I almost never do, and generally dislike—telling Mary that I had been kept awake by the fire, which I pooh-poohed as a slight accident. I had some difficulty, as a matter of fact, in preventing both her and Cook from getting excited about it. However, I managed it in the end and rested placidly most of the morning. I suppose the drug had made me a bit lazy, but in any case it was very definitely part of the spite that Edward should have a little suspense. For the same reason, too, I made Dr. Spencer send a deliberately mysterious telegram. Composing that wire was a rather delicate business.

Now I didn't want Edward to come rushing into the house and giving himself away to the maids, so I arranged to intercept him outside the front gate, but I hadn't reckoned on his deliberate attempt to run over me twice, once forwards and once backwards so to speak, and I very nearly lost my temper with him completely. I have since read over several times his account of how he thought I was a ghost haunting the place of his previous crime, and I am beginning to believe it was true and even to laugh at it, but that is only recently. At the time, and indeed until I began to write these notes, I thought it was another and most barbarous attempt. Indeed, the conviction that Edward was going to miss no chance was one of the causes that forced me to my final action, which perhaps was an unfair motive, but such is life.

At any rate I was mad with rage at the time, and rather

gave myself away in the enjoyment of pulling his leg about his luggage. Moreover, the need for a visit to Llwll that afternoon was quite imaginary.

From that time onwards a curious misunderstanding arose. I had made up my mind what action I would take if he persisted, but I had also made up my mind to be fair, and give him plenty of warning that I would not tolerate any more nonsense. When I look back on it, I still think that on numerous occasions I did give him those warnings—only of course I did not tell him what the action would be. Indeed, even from reading Edward's diary I think that the warnings were clear and obvious enough, and I might add that I think they were even more obvious than his record implies. But, amazing though it may seem, I am beginning to wonder now, when it is too late, whether he really ever understood that he was being warned.

And so things went on, I thinking that he knew that I knew and understood my hints, and he thinking that I did not know and ignoring the hints, or at any rate pretending to ignore them. But did he? Was he really so stupid? Didn't he really in his heart of hearts know more than he admitted even to himself when he wrote his accounts of what was happening? I should like to think so, I know, but really I think he did.

At any rate I thought, and I am still inclined to think, that he knew I had caught him out over the *Encyclopedia Britannica*. He couldn't tell, of course, that when he hurriedly shoved the book back on the shelf he had turned up a corner of the page and that I had read it afterwards, but surely I was clear enough for anyone? I really was alarmed when I found that he had been reading the article headed "Poison." It's nasty stuff, poison, so very difficult to provide against, and so very painful, but I was quite confident I had frightened him off it completely, and when he went off to London I genuinely hoped that the whole business was over and that I could settle down again to my own life in peace without having to be always on the look-out for Edward's little plans.

5

But while he was away I began to get nervous again.

I had noticed that he had started to be less detailed in writing his description of his future plans, and that tendency might increase. On the whole I did not think that he suspected, or was likely to suspect, that I was in the habit of reading it, but he might become superstitious about it when everything put down in it failed abysmally, or, even more likely, simply become too lazy to write any more—and then I might really be in danger.

While he was away I kept worrying and worrying over it, and over what I should have to do, if he persisted, and I didn't want to take the action he finally forced me to take, until it was no wonder that I began to make myself ill. I think that if I could have talked it over with kind Dr. Spencer it would have made all the difference, but I didn't want to involve him in my plans, and so I had to worrit it all out by myself, and, well, you must remember, when you have finished the next few pages, that I was on the verge of a breakdown.

Meanwhile, I decided to make a last attempt to clear up the situation and do what I fondly hoped would be best for everyone. It was, of course, at my suggestion that Dr. Spencer talked to Edward about making a career for himself. And, after all, how many young men wouldn't have jumped at the chance I was offering? To choose his business or profession, to have his articles or premium paid for, and an adequate allowance while he was training; was it fair that Edward should treat this with such biting scorn? Should blather about Birmingham and dungarees? I know that any office would have tried to instill some discipline into him, would have made him get up in the morning, keep office hours, and do what he was told, and I know he would have hated it, but, after all, don't most young men have to go through that sort of thing? And he was absolutely free to choose any sort of career he liked at his leisure, and go where he liked. But, perhaps, in one way he was right—no office could have stuck Edward for more than a few weeks. However, setting apart the ingratitude at the very real cost of it to me, it was downright stupid not to jump at it. Edward was always a fool as well as being a poor fish.

And so when I read his account of how he received my suggestion, my blood fairly boiled. There was, then, to be no peace. I had expected preliminary objections, but it looked as if there was no chance of his coming round to it. It boiled still more when I read his coldblooded preparations to kill me in a singularly painful way. The way that young man sat down and discussed the relative advantages of one poison over another was positively disgusting. I got angrier and angrier as he waded through prussic acid and creosote and oxalic acid, and all sorts of other things, but all the same I couldn't help laughing at him. At how his absurd attempts to buy oxalic acid resulted in his purchasing a Christmas card—at least looking at them: I think he was too mean to buy one, and I know he never sent one to anyone—oh, yes, he did buy just one—at how he funked the poison register, at how he wondered how to make this and that chemical and cursed when simple scientific language was beyond his comprehension, even at how he overate himself at lunch, but I stopped laughing when I realized that the consequences of Edward's little vendetta with me might affect all sorts of other people who were really barely concerned in the matter. He was rapidly getting to the state when he would have tried to bring in all the Spencers because they had thwarted him, Cook because she obviously "couldn't abide him," and Mary because she wouldn't become his mistress. He would have been, at the best, indifferent as to whether he killed half the inhabitants of Llwll. And that I could not allow.

However, I still gave him several more warnings, several more opportunities to drop his plan, and the door to an honorable career was still there if he chose to go through it and follow the road it opened onto. But he wouldn't.

Meanwhile, while I hoped that repentance—or if that was

too much to hope for, mere caution would restrain him,
I could not resist having a little quiet fun with him.
The real cream of the joke was that there wasn't an aconite
in the garden! I wouldn't have such a thing even if I liked it,
and as a matter of fact I'm not very fond of them. Moreover,
if there were, I have an idea that the kind one cultivates is
not "aconitum ferox," and is, though poisonous enough, nothing like so dangerous as Edward thought.

I could therefore, with safety, watch his elementary attempts at botany, and lead him almost literally "up the
garden path," and it was fun to see his back nearly breaking with the unaccustomed strain of stooping, to watch his
soft hands blistering with the use of hoe and rake—oh, yes,
Edward did a great deal more work that evening than he
admitted—and all the time it really was a disgraceful swindle
on the poor boy, for he wasn't going to get his wages for
his work.

At first I thought that I would simply keep off the subject
of aconites altogether. It would have been very easy to have
avoided giving that name to any plant as they weren't there,
and I might have managed quite easily to close down the
conversation long before we got to the plants he thought were
aconites. (They were, in fact, nothing more dangerous than
aquilegias, or columbines, if you must have the English
name of them, and Edward's description of them is not only
scientifically quite wrong, but isn't even well observed
from a lay point of view.) I might, as I say, have
stopped him quite readily by asking him to repeat what I
had already named, and when he failed—as fail he would
have done—have gone over the old ones again and ended by
saying that that was enough for one day. I did think of doing
so and extracting more gardening for more information, but
really Edward was so distressed by his exertions that I
doubted if I should ever get him to try again.

So presently I had another and brighter idea. First of all
I tested out to see if he knew anything at all. As I imagined,
he knew absolutely nothing. He swallowed quite cheerfully

the most preposterous mistakes. I could have called a rose a foxglove if I had chosen, and I did call a perfectly ordinary dahlia an erica, to which it bears not the faintest resemblance, and finally I invented lovely names like escholeria and saxifranutum, and complete nonsense like that—and Edward was apparently terribly impressed. And finally, just for fun, to ·see what would happen, I told him that a common or garden larkspur was an aconite.

It was quite a good joke. It made it safer for one thing. If Edward had learnt that there were no aconites in the garden, he might have gone out and bought some, or started some other bright plan, "something lingering with boiling oil in it." And for another, Edward's face was a study. He really gave himself away much more than he thought or pretended by asking most ridiculous questions. And his subsequent furtive attempts, most of which I watched from a distance, to find out if I was wrong, if I was deceiving him, or if I was really right after all, were too funny. I've never known anyone so ignorant, but I must admit that I thought he had swallowed my lie completely, and I now know he had his doubts. Perhaps, if he'd remember that aconites were "of the buttercup order," it might have been a better guide for him than prating about racemes and sepals which he didn't understand. Some of his experiments incidentally were most odd. He seemed to think that if you dug a plant up, examined its roots and then put it back again, it would continue to grow. It's hard to believe, but at any rate he was rapidly removing all the larkspur and columbines from the garden.

But much though I enjoyed watching this disciple of the "virile Mosley"—really, though I don't agree with him politically, I think that was a bit hard on poor Sir Oswald!—making a fool of himself botanically, the horrid fact remained that Edward was not yet cured of his desire to poison us, and a most unpleasant doubt began to assail me that perhaps the roots of larkspur, columbines, and possibly all sorts of other things mightn't be good for me. And more seriously I began

to wonder whether even when this plan had failed as igno-
miniously as the rest, Edward would abandon the unequal
struggle, and I really didn't think my health would stand it
much longer.

Accordingly, then, I decided finally to force the issue. Edward should have one last chance to start working. If he
took it, I would do my level best to help him. If he refused
and merely sulked, I would try to force him—and I think
he was right about one thing, I should have forced him in
the end to do something, though not necessarily in Birmingham. If he managed for the first time in his life to disobey
me successfully and remain at Brynmawr, but abandoned
his plans, so that life for both of us went back to what it
had been before I forced him to walk that hot summer
afternoon into Llwll and back, well, I would try to put up
with it and we would jog along somehow. But it he refused,
and, after receiving this last final warning, still continued
to attempt to carry out his design, then I should have no
mercy.

6

And so we come to the final interview.

Really, Edward's account is hardly fair. It was, perhaps,
tactless of me to select the moment when he liked to go to
sleep as the time for entering on a serious discussion, but
I never could approve or even remember this habit of his.
Besides which, he was rather inclined to deny its regularity
and to say, like so many people, that he liked a few minutes'
rest occasionally, but only if there was nothing else to do.
But to say that I delivered "a monologue, a lecture almost"
seems to me an exaggeration. All I was trying to do was
to point out to him why he really ought to try to adopt
some serious role in life, and you can see, even from his
account, that I started gently enough. By the way, I may
have stood with my "stumpy, ungainly figure" and my "feet
planted firmly apart" but, just as a matter of accuracy, they

were planted on *my* hearthrug, not on Edward's, and that was a detail which he could not remember.

Well, letting that be, Edward's attitude to what I considered, and still consider, a definitely serious offer, was anything but responsive. So far, I had kept my temper, though I must own, with difficulty, but I will allow that my tone was possibly a little stern when I said I was waiting for an answer. I intended to have one. But so far there had been no hard words; candor, certainly, but nothing bitter or cruel as yet, as Edward implies that there was.

But then Edward, to my great surprise, lost his temper completely. I had no idea how full of bottled-up spite he was, and it was more with amazement than anything else that I listened at first. But as he went on I got angry in my turn. I could put aside the frothy claptrap about "wage slaves" and the silly remarks about being freed of his keep— even Edward must have realized that I was offering to spend more money on him than I had been doing in the past—but I would not stand his rude references to dear Dr. Spencer, a man without whose care Edward would never have been reared. And when finally Edward, with a reference to his Pekingese, threw in my teeth his own attempt to kill me, I came to the conclusion that it was time for plain speaking, for making one last attempt to warn him from his course of self-destruction, and, as he says, I reminded him of the mess he had made of his boyhood and his life generally—and, believe me, Edward's diary has a remarkable trick of softening down his actions, and nowhere does he do it more neatly than when he describes his expulsion from school. Well, on that, and on many other points, I spoke out, and I will acknowledge I spoke heatedly, but I do deny that I "slated him like a fishwife," even if I did use a telling phrase or two.

And finally, did I not end by warning him clearly? He was to behave himself, and this time he did know what I meant. He was to behave himself or I should take action.

And so, when he failed completely and utterly to behave

himself, I did take action. What else could I do? I could not let things stay as they were. It was not only a question of danger to myself. There was danger for everyone else at Brynmawr, and even in Llwll, while Edward was able to go on with plan after plan; for, futile though his plans were, it was almost a certainty that one day one of his crude attempts would come off. Nor could I take anyone into my confidence, and least of all could I allow any scandal to fall on the name of the Powells of Brynmawr. For some centuries we had lived there; if Edward and I were the last of them we should not end with Edward being hanged for murdering me. Nor could I quite trust Edward to carry on the family name without my control.

But it is time for me to cease my commentary on Edward's diary and to conclude what he necessarily left unfinished. There are one or two details I shall leave out or intentionally confuse, in the same way that I have confused small points, names, geography and so on, when editing what Edward wrote, so that inquisitive people may not take too great an interest in what does not concern them.

Well then, that evening was grim. Edward would not speak to me and I, after a fruitless attempt, abandoned the effort. Besides, I had just had a slight shock. For the last few weeks, as Edward had noticed, I had avoided roast beef. Just before dinner, however, Mary had come to me with a message that the butcher had been unable to send the mutton I had asked for—he had none ready for immediate cooking—and so he had sent in a sirloin, "having noticed, ma'am, that you haven't had one for some little while; and Evans brought up the horseradish this afternoon." I only hoped that Edward did not know of it. I thanked Mary, politely enough, I hope, but now that things were coming to a crisis, I began to wonder if my nerves were equal to dealing with whatever might arise.

I slept badly that night and that was why, I suppose, I was woken so easily by the noise of Edward's alarum clock. For some minutes I lay there, puzzled, as one is when one is awakened up suddenly, until it dawned on me what the noise was. Then I got up and quickly put on some clothes.

Quietly I peered round the curtain and looked out on the wonderful country of the Welsh border. In front of me the Broad Mountain was heaving its wooded sides out of the morning mist. Over the top of it, as I looked at it, the edge of the sun was just beginning to appear, while the feet of the long hill were still shrouded in the white fleece that comes up nightly from the river. To my right, the sheep were stirring on Yr Allt and cropping the short grass shining with the morning dew. To my left the trees of the Fron Wood were beginning to take on here and there the tinges of autumn. It was a morning to rejoice in, in which life was good to live and all the world should be friends, and in front of me on the green lawn, going to my carefully tended flower-beds, driving away my white pigeons and frightening an inquisitive water-wagtail, was Edward, going to get, not flowers, but roots—a nice morning bouquet!

As he went, he gave a look up at my window, and at that moment I decided I was right in the action I proposed to take. It was the look of a madman, the look his father must have had when he and Edward's mother met that accident I never have really believed was an accident. Taking care that I made no movement that he could see, I slipped away from the window and into Edward's room. In a few seconds I was possessed of the diary. I had all along determined to have that, in case it was necessary for my own protection. With grim satisfaction I noticed his preparations for instant flight. Then I went out to the garage. I am by no means such a fool about cars as Edward would have you believe and I made the little arrangements I had planned quickly and efficiently. "La Joyeuse"—to use Edward's disgusting name— would only go as I desired it to.

Then I went back to the kitchen and waited. My first care was to see that Edward had not already mingled with the horseradish roots the things he had just carefully been digging up. I should not have been surprised if he had, because, though I had been rapid, it really oughtn't to have taken him so long. It was some time before I know what the delay was, but afterwards I discovered that tho silly boy, in his uncertainty of which plant really was an aconite, had been wandering round the garden selecting bits here and there of all sorts of things. Hence it was that I reached the kitchen first. But I had barely done so when I heard footsteps coming softly through the hall and Edward, with his shoes in one hand and a bunch of goodness knows what roots in the other, appeared.

On the whole I had decided to catch him absolutely red-handed and frighten him thoroughly; and so I waited until he was just about to mix the two bunches before I stepped out from behind the scullery door.

He was quite frightened enough. He jumped into the air and gave a sort of strangled scream—fortunately it did not wake any of the household—and bolted. In a very few seconds he was down the stairs again, so quickly that I was glad I had decided to make my arrangements before frightening him instead of after. Carefully I removed his roots and put them in the incinerator. Soon afterwards I heard the door of his car being shut and the noise of it moving cautiously off down the drive. Very quickly, and rather sadly, I went up to the window that overlooked the road in front of the house, and the point where I had crashed into the dingle.

As Edward reached there, I could see his hand go down to the brakelever or the gears, and next second something happened. Down, down the steep slope into the bottom of the dingle crashed Edward and his car, turning over and over as it went, and bursting into flames. One suit-case was thrown clear, but practically nothing else was left of Edward or his car.

I have now only to add a title to these notes, and the one I have chosen perhaps needs a word of explanation. Well, "of" can be possessive, can't it? Can mean "of or belonging to."